THE VAMPIRE PRINCE

THE SAGA OF DARREN SHAN
BOOK 6

Other titles by
DARREN SHAN

THE SAGA OF DARREN SHAN

THE DEMONATA

Also available on audio

DARREN SHAN

THE VAMPIRE PRINCE

THE SAGA OF DARREN SHAN
BOOK 6

HarperCollins *Children's Books*

If your trip to Vampire Mountain leaves you bloodthirsty for more, visit www.darrenshan.com

First published in Great Britain by HarperCollins *Children's Books* 2002
This edition published 2009
HarperCollins *Children's Books* is a division of HarperCollins*Publishers* Ltd,
77-85 Fulham Palace Road, Hammersmith,
London W6 8JB

The HarperCollins website address is:
www.harpercollins.co.uk

1

Text copyright © 2002 Darren Shan

ISBN-13 978 0 00 794554 2

The author asserts the moral right to
be identified as the author of the work.

Printed and bound in England by
Clays Ltd, St Ives plc

For:

Martha & Bill - who fed a hungry half-vampire

OBEs (Order of the Bloody Entrails) to:
Katherine "kill-crazy" Tyacke
Stella "stabber" Paskins

Editors extraordinaire:
Gillie Russell & Zoë Clarke

Agent provocateur:
Christopher Little

PROLOGUE

BE CAREFUL who you trust. Even a supposedly close friend might be capable of betraying you. I found that out the hard way.

My name's Darren Shan. I'm a half-vampire. I was blooded when I was very young, and for eight years I toured the world with the Cirque Du Freak — a travelling circus of magically gifted performers. Then my mentor – Larten Crepsley – said I had to be presented to the Vampire Princes.

Most of the Princes and Vampire Generals gathered in the remote Vampire Mountain once every twelve years, for the Council of Vampires. After a long, tiring trek to the mountain with Mr Crepsley, Harkat Mulds (a Little Person who'd been brought back from the dead by a powerful man called Mr Tiny), Gavner Purl (a General) and four wolves (including a male I called Streak and a cub I nicknamed Rudi), I faced the Princes, who said I had to prove myself worthy of joining the ranks of the undead. They set me a series of harsh tests known as the Trials of Initiation. If I passed all five tests, I'd be accepted as one of them. If I failed, I'd be killed.

I passed the first three Trials, but the fourth ended disastrously — I fell foul of a wild boar and would have been gouged to death if not for Harkat, who leapt into the pit and killed the boar. The problem was, his intervention broke all the rules. While the vampires debated my fate, one sneaked into my cell and led me away to safety. He was a blond, slender, peaceful, highly intelligent vampire called Kurda Smahlt, and he was shortly due to become a Prince. I believed he was my friend.

While we were escaping, Gavner caught up with us and tried talking me into going back to face the verdict of the Princes. Kurda persuaded him to let me go. But, as we were closing in on freedom, we ran into a bunch of vampaneze — purple-skinned adversaries of the vampires, who kill humans when they drink from them — hiding in a cave.

That's when Kurda showed his true colours. He stabbed and killed Gavner, and I realized he was in league with the vampaneze. He tried taking me alive, but I ran and fell into a mountain stream. Kurda would have saved me, but I ignored his helping hand and surrendered myself to the vicious flow of the stream, which swiftly swept me away underground, into the belly of the mountain and certain death...

CHAPTER ONE

DARKNESS — COLD — churning water — roaring, like a thousand lions — spinning around and around — bashing into rocks — arms wrapped around my face to protect it — tucking up legs to make myself smaller, less of a target.

Wash up against a mass of roots — grab hold — slippery — the wet roots feel like dead fingers clutching at me — a gap between the water and the roof of the tunnel — I draw quick gasps of breath — current takes hold again — try fighting it — roots break off in my hands — swept away.

Tumbling over and over — hit my head hard on a rock — see stars — almost black out — struggle to keep head up — spit water out of my mouth, but more gushes in — feels like I'm swallowing half the stream.

The current drags me against a wall — sharp rocks cut deeply into my thighs and hips — freezing cold water numbs the pain — stops the flow of blood — a sudden drop —

plummet into a deep pool — down, down, down — held under by force of the falling water — panicking — can't find my way up — drowning — if I don't break free soon, I'll…

My feet strike a wall and propel me forward — drift slowly up and away from the pool — flow is gentle here — lots of space between water and top of tunnel — able to bob along and breathe — air's cold, and it stings my lungs, but I gulp it down thankfully.

The stream opens out into what sounds like a large cave. Roars from the opposite end: the water must drop sharply again there. I let myself drift to one side before facing the drop. I need to rest and fill my lungs with air. As I tread water near the wall in the dark, something clutches at my bald head. It feels like twigs. I grab at them to steady myself, then realize they're not twigs — they're *bones!*

Too exhausted to be scared, I grasp the bones as though they were part of a lifebuoy. Taking long, deep breaths, I explore the bones with my fingers. They connect to a wrist, an arm, a body and head: a full skeleton. This stream was used to dispose of dead vampires in the past. This one must have washed up here and rotted away over the decades. I search blindly for other skeletons but find none. I wonder who the vampire was, when he lived, how long he's been here. It must be horrible, trapped in a cave like this, no proper burial, no final resting place.

I give the skeleton a shake, hoping to free it. The cave erupts with high-pitched screeches and flapping sounds. Wings! Dozens or hundreds of pairs of wings! Something crashes into my face and catches on my left ear. It scratches and nips. I yelp, tear it loose and slap it away.

I can't see anything, but I sense a flurry of objects flying over and around me. Another collides with me. This time I hold on and feel around it — a *bat*! The cave's full of bats. They must nest here, in the roof. The sound of me shaking the skeleton disturbed them, and they've taken flight.

I don't panic. They won't attack me. They're just frightened and will settle down soon. I release the one I've caught and let it join the rush above me. The noise dies down after a few minutes and the bats return to their perches. Silence.

I wonder how they get in and out of the cave. There must be a crack in the roof. For a few seconds I dream about finding it and climbing to safety, but my numb fingers and toes quickly put an end to thoughts of that nature. I couldn't climb, even if I could find the crack and it was big enough for me to fit through.

I start thinking about the skeleton again. I don't want to leave it here. I tug at it, careful this time not to create a racket. It doesn't budge at first — it's wedged firm. I get a stronger grip and pull again. It comes loose, all at once, and falls on top of me, driving me under. Water gushes down my throat. *Now* I panic! The skeleton heavy on top of me, weighing me down. I'm going to drown! I'm going to drown! I'm going to—

No! Stop panicking. Use my brain. I wrap my arms around the skeleton and slowly roll over. It works! Now the skeleton's underneath and I'm on top. The air tastes good.

My heart stops pounding. A few of the bats are circling again, but most are still.

Releasing the skeleton, I guide it out towards the middle of the cave, using my feet. I feel the current take it, then it's gone. I hang on to the wall, treading water, giving the skeleton time to wash ahead of me. I fall to thinking while I wait: was it a good idea to free the skeleton? A nice gesture, but if the bones snag on a rock further along and block my way…

Too late to worry now. Should have thought of that before.

My situation's as desperate as ever. Crazy to think I might get out of this alive. But I force myself to think positively: I've made it this far, and the stream must open up sooner or later. Who's to say I can't make it to the end? Believe, Darren, *believe.*

I'd like to hang here forever – easier to cling on and die of the cold – but I've got to try for freedom. In the end, I force my fingers to unclench and let go of the bank. I drift out into the middle of the stream. The current bites at me and latches on. Speeding up — the exit — roaring grows furiously — flowing fast — angling sharply downwards — gone.

CHAPTER TWO

Even worse beyond the cave — makes the first half of the ride seem like a paddle in a swimming pool — sickening drops and turns — walls studded with jagged stones — water gushes wildly, madly — tossed about as though made of putty — impossible to exert control — no time to pause for breath — lungs bursting — hold my arms tight over my head — tuck my legs up as far as they'll go — conserve oxygen — bash my head on rocks — my back — legs — belly — back — head — shoulders — head…

Lose count of the collisions — can't feel pain any longer — eyes playing tricks on me — looking up, it's as if the rocks are invisible — I believe I can see the sky, the stars, the moon — this is the beginning of the end — senses in disarray, brain shutting down — out of luck — out of hope — out of life.

I open my mouth to take one long, last drink of water —

slam into a wall — air explodes out of me — force of crash pops me upwards — I break through to a small pocket of air between water and roof — lungs draw it in greedily, automatically.

I float here a few seconds, pressed against wall, gasping in air — current takes me again and drags me under — through a narrow tunnel — incredible speed — like a bullet — tunnel getting narrower — speed increases — my back scrapes along the wall — the rock's smooth, otherwise I'd be cut to shreds — feels like a water slide — almost enjoying this part of the nightmarish ride.

Tunnel evens out — running low on oxygen again — try forcing head up, to search for air — can't — don't have the energy to fight.

Water creeps up my nose — I cough — water pours down my throat — I'm losing the battle — roll over, face down — this is the end — lungs are filling with water — I can't close my mouth — waiting for death — all of a sudden: no water — flying — (*flying?*) — whistling air surrounds me — looking down at land — stream cutting through it — floating, as though I'm a bird or a bat — closer to stream — closer — are my eyes playing tricks again?

Turn over in middle of flight — look up — sky, *real* sky, open and bright with stars — beautiful — *I'm out!* — I'm really out! — I made it! — I can breathe! I'm alive! I'm...

Flight ends — hit water hard — impact shakes my guts to pieces and knocks brain out of order — blackness again, only this time inside my head.

CHAPTER THREE

CONSCIOUSNESS RETURNS gradually. Sounds strike me first: the roar of the water, much softer than in the mountain, almost lyrical. Slowly, my eyes flutter open. I'm staring up at stars, drifting along on my back. Luck or my body's natural defences? I don't know. I don't care. I'm *alive!*

The current isn't strong here. I could easily swim to the bank, pull myself to safety and begin the trip back to Vampire Mountain, which I spot in the near distance. Except I don't have the strength. I try rolling over to swim — can't. My legs and arms are like dead blocks of wood. I've survived the ride through the mountain, but the cost has been high. I'm completely limp and helpless.

I study the landscape while the stream sweeps me further away from Vampire Mountain. It's rugged and unspectacular, but beautiful after the darkness. *Anything* would seem beautiful after the darkness. I'll never take the countryside for granted again.

Am I dying? I could be — no feeling, no control, at the mercy of the stream. Maybe I'm dead already and just haven't realized it. No! Not dead. Water splashes up my nose and I splutter: proof I'm still alive. I won't give up, not after all I've been through. I have to summon strength from somewhere and make it to the bank. I can't drift along like this forever: the longer it drags on, the harder it will be.

I try willing energy into my exhausted limbs. I think about dying young and what a waste it would be, but that doesn't give me strength. I think about the vampires and the threat they face from Kurda and the vampaneze, but that doesn't work either. Finally, an old vampire myth succeeds in spreading a burst of fire through my icy bones: I recall the myth that a vampire who dies in running water is doomed to stick around as a ghost — no journey to Paradise for those who die in rivers or streams.

Strangely (as I never believed the myth), the thought spurs me into action. I raise a weak arm and flap feebly for the bank. The action doesn't do much, apart from spin me round a little, but the fact that I'm able to move at all fills me with hope.

Gritting my teeth, I face the bank and force my legs up behind me. They respond sluggishly, but they *do* respond. I try to swim freestyle — can't. I roll over on to my back, kick weakly with my feet, and guide myself with gentle hand motions. I slowly pull towards the bank. It takes a long time, and I'm swept much further away from Vampire Mountain, but finally I'm in shallow water, out of the current.

I half rise to my knees, then collapse. Lying face down, I turn my head sideways, splutter, then get back on my knees. I crawl out of the water, on to the snowy bank, where I collapse again. My eyes close. I weep silently into the snow.

I want to lie here and freeze: simpler than moving. But my feet are still in the water and I don't like the feel of them drifting behind me, so I pull them clear. The effort goads me into further action. Groaning, I prop myself up, then rise slowly and painfully to my feet.

Standing, I stare around as if I'm on an alien planet. Everything looks different. Day is breaking, but stars and the moon still shine lightly in the sky. After so long inside the mountain, I'd forgotten what daylight looks like. It's wonderful. I could stand here all day and just stare, except that wouldn't get me anywhere, and soon I'd fall, into the stream or the snow, and freeze.

Sighing, obeying some insistent inner instinct, I drag my feet forward a few steps, pause, shake my head, straighten up and lurch away from the stream, which froths and hisses angrily behind me — cheated of its victim.

CHAPTER FOUR

IT DIDN'T take me long to realize I couldn't make it very far if I continued in this state. I was soaked to the skin. My clothes were heavy with water and the air around me was bitterly cold. Mr Crepsley had warned me what to do if this ever happened: get rid of the wet clothes swiftly, or I'd freeze to death inside them.

It took a lot of effort to get out of my clothes. My fingers were numb and I ended up having to use my teeth to tear my way free. But I felt better when I'd undressed. A great weight had been lifted from my body, and though the full force of the cold hit me immediately, I set forward at a brisker pace.

It didn't bother me that I was wandering around as naked as the animals of the wild. There was nobody to see. Even if there had been, I wouldn't have cared — being so close to death, modesty was the last thing on my mind.

My brisk pace didn't last long. After a while, I began to

understand just how serious a mess I was in. I was stranded in the middle of nowhere, no clothes to protect me from the cold, beaten to a pulp, physically and mentally drained, with nothing to eat. It was a struggle just to keep moving. In a matter of minutes, I'd run out of energy and collapse. The cold would set in. Frostbite and hypothermia would finish me off.

I tried jogging, to warm myself up, but couldn't. My legs simply wouldn't work. It was a miracle they were able to support me at all. Anything faster than a slow crawl was beyond them.

I stopped and turned in a full circle, hoping to spot something familiar. If I was close to one of the resting places known as way-stations, used by vampires on their way to and from Council, there might be hope. I could hole-up, catch a day or two of sleep, and recover my strength. A good plan, with just one major flaw — I hadn't a clue where I was or if there were any way-stations nearby.

I weighed up my options. Standing still would get me nowhere. And scouting for a way-station was out of the question — I hadn't the strength or time. The first order of the day was to find somewhere sheltered to recuperate. Food, warmth and working my way back to Vampire Mountain could come later — *if* I survived.

There was a forest about a kilometre to my left. That was the best place to head. I could curl up at the base of a tree and cover myself with leaves. Maybe find some insects or small animals to feed upon. It wasn't ideal, but it made more sense than standing here in the open, or climbing slippery rocks in search of caves.

I fell many times on my way to the forest. That wasn't surprising — I was amazed I'd made it this far. Each time I lay in the snow a few minutes, gathering my diminished resources, then hauled myself to my feet and staggered on again.

The forest had assumed magical properties. I was convinced, if I could make it to the trees, everything would be fine. Deep inside, I knew that was nonsense, but the belief kept me going. Without it, I'd have been unable to continue.

I finally ran out of steam a hundred metres or less from the first trees of the forest. I knew in my heart, as I lay panting in the snow, that I'd reached the end of my tether. All the same, I rested a few minutes, as I had before, then made a valiant effort to rise — no good. I made it as far as my knees, then dropped. Another long rest. Again I tried to rise. Again I fell, this time face first into the snow, where I lay, shivering, unable to roll over.

The cold was unbearable. A human would have died from it long ago. Only the vampire blood inside my veins had kept me going. But even the powerful blood of the vampires had its limits. I'd pushed to the very end of mine. I'd no strength left, not even the tiniest morsel.

I was finished.

I wept pitifully as I lay there, tears turning to ice on my cheeks. Snowflakes drifted on to my eyelashes. I tried lifting a hand to brush them away, but couldn't. Even that small gesture was beyond me. "What an awful way to die," I moaned. Another hundred metres and I would have been safe. To collapse and die this close to the end was a shame. Maybe if I'd rested more in the cave in the mountain, I'd have had the energy to continue. Or if I'd—

A sharp, yapping sound jolted me out of my reverie. I'd closed my eyes and had been drifting off to sleep/death. At the sound, I cracked them open. I couldn't move my head, and the flakes of snow clouded my vision, but I was staring in the general direction of the forest and could see a vague shape making its way towards me, tumbling through the snow. Oh, great, I thought sarcastically. As if things weren't bad enough — now something's going to come along and eat me before I'm dead! Could things get any worse? Judging by what had happened to me recently — *yes!*

I shut my eyes as the creature came nearer and hoped I'd be too numb to feel its teeth and claws as it devoured me. Fighting back was out of the question — a squirrel could have knocked the stuffing out of me, the condition I was in.

Hot breath clouded my face. A long tongue licked around my nose. I shivered. It licked again, this time my cheeks and ears. Then it licked the snowflakes from my eyelashes.

I opened my eyes and blinked. What was going on? Was it cleaning me up before it killed me? That seemed unlikely. Yet what other explanation could there be? As I adjusted my vision, the animal nudged back a bit and came into focus. My jaw dropped. My lips quivered. And in a pained, shaky voice, I mumbled incredulously: *"Rudi?"*

CHAPTER FIVE

RUDI WAS the wolf cub who'd accompanied Mr Crepsley, Harkat, Gavner and me on some of the way to Vampire Mountain. He'd been part of a small pack, which included two she-wolves and a large male whom I'd christened Streak. They'd left us to unite with other wolf packs close to Vampire Mountain.

Rudi leapt around me, barking with excitement. He'd grown a bit since I'd last seen him: his fangs were longer and his fur was thicker than ever. I managed to lift my head and smile weakly. "I'm in big trouble, Rudi," I muttered as the cub licked my fingers. He cocked his ears and gazed at me seriously, as though he understood. "Big trouble," I repeated softly, then collapsed again.

Rudi rubbed his nose against my right cheek. It was wet and warm. He licked around my eyes and ears, then pressed his body against mine, trying to warm me up. When he saw how helpless I was, he took a few paces back and howled. Moments later, a second wolf emerged from the forest, larger, sleeker, every bit as familiar as Rudi.

"Streak," I whispered as the wolf advanced cautiously. His ears perked up when he heard my voice, then he bounded forward. Rudi carried on yapping until Streak snapped at him. The adult wolf sniffed me from head to toe, then barked at Rudi. They lay out flat beside me, Streak behind, Rudi in front, covering most of my body with theirs, transmitting their heat.

After a few minutes, warmth seeped through me. I flexed and unflexed my fingers and toes, working the worst of the chill out of them. I curled up into a ball, so the wolves could cover more of me, and buried my face between Rudi's hairy shoulders. We lay like that for ages, the wolves shifting position every so often to keep warm. Finally, Streak got to his feet and barked.

I tried getting up. Failed. Shook my head and groaned. "It's no use. I can't go on." The wolf studied me silently, then bent and bit my bum! I yelped and rolled away instinctively. Streak followed and I leapt to my feet. "Stay back, you no-good—" I shouted, then stopped when I saw the look on his face.

I stared down at my body, then at Streak, and grinned sheepishly. "I'm standing," I whispered redundantly. Streak howled softly, then nipped my right leg lightly and faced the trees. Nodding wearily, I set off for the forest and the wolves padded along beside me.

The going wasn't easy. I was cold and exhausted, and stumbled more times than I could keep track of. Streak and Rudi kept me going. Whenever I stalled, they pressed against me, or breathed warmly over me, or snapped to make me get up. At one stage, Streak let me grab the thick, long hair around his neck, and half-dragged me through the snow.

I'm not sure why they bothered with me — normally wild animals leave wounded companions behind if they can't keep up. Maybe they wanted to keep on the good side of the vampires, who put lots of scraps their way during Council. Or perhaps they sensed hidden resources within me and knew my cause wasn't hopeless.

After a long, hard walk, we entered a glade, where a large pack of wolves had gathered. There must have been twenty or thirty of the predators, lying about, eating, playing and grooming themselves, all different colours, builds and breeds. The wolves regarded me with suspicion. One, a dark, bulky male, padded over and sniffed me, then growled threateningly, raising its hackles. Streak met its challenge and growled back. The two stood snarling at each other for a few seconds, before the unwelcoming wolf turned its back on us and loped away.

Rudi ran after the dark wolf, yapping, but Streak barked angrily at the cub and he returned, tail between his legs. As I blinked owlishly at the wolves, Streak nudged me forward to where a she-wolf was suckling three cubs. She laid a protective paw over her cubs and growled at us as we approached, but Streak whined and dropped to his belly to show he meant no harm.

When the she-wolf had relaxed, Streak stood and locked gazes with the female. The she-wolf snarled. Streak bared his fangs and snarled back, pawed at the snow in front of her, then locked gazes again. This time, she lowered her head and didn't respond. Streak struck the backs of my legs with his snout and I dropped to the ground. As he nudged me on, I understood what he wanted me to do. "No!" I resisted, insides churning. "I can't!"

Streak growled and pushed me forward. I was too weak to argue. Besides, it made sense — I was cold and hungry, but too weak to eat. I needed to get something warm and nourishing down me, something that didn't need to be chewed.

I lay down and wriggled forward, gently shoving the three cubs to one side, making space. The cubs yapped suspiciously at me, then crowded round, sniffed me all over, and accepted me as one of their own. When my face was up close to the suckling she-wolf's belly, I took a deep breath, paused momentarily, then found a milk-engorged teat, closed my lips around it, and drank.

CHAPTER SIX

THE SHE-WOLF treated me the same as the three cubs, making sure I got enough milk, covering me with her paws to keep me warm, licking behind my ears and around my face to clean me (I crept away when I had to go to the toilet!). I remained with her for a couple of days, slowly regaining my strength, cuddling up to her and the cubs for warmth, surviving on her warm milk. It didn't taste good, but I was in no position to complain.

Pain racked my body as I recovered. Bruises covered every last scrap of me. My cuts weren't too serious — the cold restricted the flow of blood — but they stung like mad. I wished I had some of Seba's healing spider webs to apply to them.

The more I thought about my slide down the mountain stream, the more incredible it seemed. Had I really done it, or was this some crazy dream? If not for the pain, I might have believed it was the latter, but dreams are painless, so it had to be real.

More incredible still was that I hadn't broken any major bones. Three fingers on my left hand were broken, my right thumb was sticking out at an alarming angle, and my left ankle had blown up like a purple balloon, but otherwise I seemed to be OK. I could move my arms and legs; my skull hadn't been cracked open; my backbone hadn't been snapped in two. All things considered, I was in astoundingly good shape.

As the days passed, I stretched and tested myself. I still slept beside the she-wolf and drank from her, but I started getting up to take short walks, hobbling around the glade, exercising lightly. My left ankle pained me terribly, but the swelling subsided gradually and eventually returned to normal.

As my strength returned, Streak brought me meat and berries. I couldn't eat a lot in the beginning, but I sucked plenty of blood from the small animals he brought, and my appetite increased swiftly.

Rudi spent a lot of time with me. He was fascinated by my bald head — I'd had to shave my hair off after it caught fire during one of my Trials of Initiation — and never tired of licking it and rubbing his chin and nose over it.

After four days (possibly five or six — I hadn't kept a clear track of time) the wolves moved on to a new patch. It was a long march — seven or eight kilometres — and I lagged behind most of the way, helped along by Streak, Rudi and the she-wolf who'd been suckling me (she now regarded me as one of her cubs, and mothered me the same as the others).

As punishing as the trek was, it was beneficial, and when I awoke that night after a long, dreamless sleep, I felt almost as good as I had before my descent down the stream. The worst of the bruising had subsided, the cuts had healed, my ankle barely troubled me, and I was able to eat normally.

That night, I went hunting with the pack. I couldn't move fast, but I kept up, and helped bring down an old reindeer that several of the wolves were tracking. It felt good to be contributing to the pack after they'd done so much for me, and I gave most of my share of the meat to the she-wolf and cubs.

There was a nasty scene the next day. The dark wolf who'd objected to my presence when Streak brought me into the pack had never accepted me. He growled and barked whenever I came close, and often snatched food from my hands while I was feeding. I avoided him as much as I could, but that day, when he saw me playing with the cubs and handing meat out to them, he snapped.

He charged at me, barking wildly, meaning to drive me off. I backed away from him slowly, not showing any fear, but I didn't leave the pack — if I let him chase me out once, he'd never stop hounding me. I circled around the wolves, hoping he'd lose interest in me, but he followed, determined, snarling menacingly.

As I prepared to fight, Streak darted between us and faced the darker wolf. He raised his hackles to make himself look big, and growled deeply. It looked as though the dark wolf would back off, but then he lowered his head, bared his fangs and lunged at Streak, claws extended.

Streak met the challenge and the pair rolled away, biting and scratching at one another. The wolves around them hastily cleared out of their way. Some younger cubs yapped with excitement, but most of the older wolves ignored the fighting or looked on with only mild interest. They were accustomed to quarrels like this.

It seemed to me as though the wolves were going to tear each other to bits, and I ran around them worriedly, hoping to prise them apart. But as the fight progressed, I realized that, for all their barking, snapping and clawing, they weren't doing a lot of actual damage. Streak's snout had been scratched, and the dark wolf was bleeding from a couple of bites, but they weren't out to really hurt each other. It was more like a wrestling match than anything else.

As the fight wore on, it became obvious that Streak had the beating of the other wolf. He wasn't as heavily built, but he was faster and sharper, and for every swipe to the head he took, he delivered two or three of his own.

All of a sudden, the dark wolf stopped, lay down and rolled over, baring his throat and belly. Streak opened his mouth and clamped his teeth around the dark wolf's throat, then let go without breaking the skin and stood back. The dark wolf got to his feet and slunk away, tail between his legs.

I thought the wolf might have to leave the pack, but he didn't. Although he slept by himself that night, none of the wolves tried to chase him away, and he took his regular place in the hunting pack the next time they set out.

I thought about that a lot over the next day or two, comparing the way wolves handled their losers with how vampires handled theirs. In the world of vampires, defeat was a disgrace, and more often than not ended with the death of the defeated. Wolves were more understanding. Honour mattered to them, but they wouldn't kill or shun a member of their pack just because it had lost face. Young wolf cubs had to endure tests of maturity, just as I'd endured the Trials of Initiation, but they weren't killed if they failed.

I wasn't an expert on the subject, but it seemed to me that vampires could learn a thing or two from wolves if they took the time to study their ways. It *was* possible to be both honourable and practical. Kurda Smahlt, for all his treacherous faults, got that much right at least.

CHAPTER SEVEN

A FEW more days slipped by. I was so glad to be alive, I was savouring every moment of it. My body had healed almost completely, though faint bruises lingered in certain places. My strength had returned. I was full of vim and vinegar (one of my Dad's expressions; I never figured out what it actually meant), raring to go.

I took hardly any notice of the cold. I'd grown used to the nip of the wind and the chill of the snow. The occasional strong blast set me shivering, but most of the time I felt as natural wandering about naked as the wolves.

I'd been accepted as an equal member of the pack now that I was back on my feet, and I was constantly out hunting — since I was able to run faster than the wolves, my services were in great demand. I was gradually coming to terms with the way they thought and communicated. I couldn't read their thoughts but most of the time I had a good idea what they were thinking — I could tell by the way they hunched their shoulders, widened or narrowed their eyes, perked or dropped their ears and tails, growled or barked or whined. On the hunt, if Streak or another wolf wanted me to go to the left or the right, they only had to look at me and twitch their heads. If a she-wolf wanted me to play with her cubs, she howled in a certain soft way, and I knew she was calling me.

The wolves, for their part, seemed able to understand everything I said. I rarely spoke – there wasn't much need for words – but whenever I did, they'd cock their heads intently and listen, then reply with a yap or gesture.

We moved around a lot, as was the wolfen way. I kept an eye open for Vampire Mountain, but didn't spot it. That puzzled me — the reason the wolves met out here in the wilds was to converge on the mountain and eat the leftovers that the vampires threw to them. I decided to ask Streak about it, though I didn't think he'd be able to comprehend my question or fashion a reply. To my surprise, when I mentioned Vampire Mountain, the hackles rose on the back of his neck and he growled.

"You don't want to go there?" I frowned. "Why not?" Streak's only reply was another growl. Thinking about it, I guessed it had to be the vampaneze. The wolves must know about the purple-skinned invaders, or else they'd simply sensed trouble and were steering clear of the mountain.

I had to do something about the vampaneze, but the thought of going back to Vampire Mountain scared me. I was afraid the vampires would kill me before I had a chance to explain about the vampaneze. Or they might think I was lying and take Kurda's word over mine. Eventually I'd have to return, but I was delaying as long as possible, pretending to myself that I was still recovering and not fit to make the trip.

My three broken fingers had mended. I'd set the bones as best I could – *very* painful! – and wrapped the fingers together using long reeds and leaves. The thumb on my right hand still stuck out at an angle and hurt when I moved it, but that was only a minor irritation.

When I wasn't hunting or playing with the cubs, I thought a lot about Gavner. I got a pain in my belly whenever I recalled his death, but I couldn't stop thinking about him. The loss of a friend is a terrible, tragic thing, especially when it happens suddenly, without warning.

What really sickened me about Gavner's death was that it could have been avoided. If I hadn't run away, or if I hadn't trusted Kurda, or if I'd stayed and fought with Gavner — he'd still be alive. It wasn't fair. He didn't deserve to die. He'd been a brave, loyal, warm-hearted vampire, a friend to all.

Sometimes, when I thought about him, I was filled with hatred and wished I'd grabbed his knife and killed Kurda, even if it meant my own death at the hands of the vampaneze. Other times, a sweeping sadness would come over me and I'd cover my face with my hands and cry, wondering what prompted Kurda to do such an awful thing.

The wolves were puzzled by my behaviour. They didn't spend much time grieving for their dead. If they lost a partner or cub, they howled miserably for a while, then got on with their lives. They couldn't understand my mood swings.

To cheer me up, Streak took me out hunting with him late one evening. Normally, we never went hunting by ourselves, but the pack was settling in for the night, so we went without them.

It was nice to be on our own. A drawback to running with a pack is that you have to be very organized — if you make a wrong move that ruins the hunt, you're treated with disgust. Now that it was just Streak and me, we were free to lollop along as we pleased and make idle detours. It didn't matter whether we caught something or not — we were in search of sport, not prey.

We tracked a couple of young, frisky reindeer. We didn't expect to catch them, but it was fun to follow them. I think they sensed our harmless intentions because they kept turning back and running at us, then tossing their heads and fleeing. We'd been tracking them for almost a quarter of an hour when the two reindeer reached the top of a small mound and paused to sniff the air. I started after them, but Streak growled and drew to a halt.

I stopped, wondering what was wrong. Streak was standing stock-still like the reindeer. Then, as the reindeer turned and bolted back towards us, he nudged my legs with his snout and took off for a clump of bushes to the side. I followed quickly, trusting his more highly developed senses. We found a thick bush which afforded us a clear view of the mound, and lay low behind it.

A minute passed. Two. Then a figure appeared over the mound. My eyes were as sharp as they'd ever been, and I recognized the far-off vampire immediately — *Mr Crepsley!*

I started to get to my feet, overjoyed, and opened my mouth to roar a greeting. A low growl from Streak stopped me. The wolf's tail hung flat behind him, the way it did when he was anxious. I wanted to rush forward to greet my old friend, but I knew Streak wouldn't be acting this way without good reason.

Lying down flat beside the wolf, I kept my eyes on the mound, and soon the cause for his concern became obvious: behind Mr Crepsley marched five other vampires, and at the fore, carrying a sharp, polished sword, was the would-be Prince and traitor — *Kurda Smahlt!*

CHAPTER EIGHT

I KEPT close to the ground as the vampires passed, hidden behind the bushes, downwind so they couldn't smell me. Once they were out of immediate range, I turned to Streak. "We have to follow them," I whispered. Streak studied me in silence with his large, yellow eyes, then got to his feet. He slipped further back through the bushes. I trailed after him, trusting him not to lead me astray. A few minutes later, we circled around and caught sight of the vampires. We fell in behind them and matched their pace, careful not to get too close.

I examined the four vampires with Mr Crepsley and Kurda. Three were unfamiliar, but the fourth was Arra Sails. Her right arm had been in a sling the last time I saw her, but it was now hanging freely by her side. After a while, I noticed that two of the unfamiliar vampires were carrying swords like Kurda's, and were lagging a bit behind Arra and the other unarmed vampire.

It became clear what was happening. Mr Crepsley had decided to come looking for me. Arra and the other vampire had agreed to accompany him. Kurda, worried that I might have somehow survived, must have offered to assist, and brought the armed vampires with him. If they discovered me alive, the swords would flash, and that would be the end of myself, Mr Crepsley, Arra and the other vampire. Kurda was making sure word of his betrayal never made it back to the Generals and Princes.

I wasn't surprised by Kurda's devious plotting, but I was upset by the realization that he wasn't the only traitor. The two vampires with swords must have known the truth about him and the vampaneze, otherwise he wouldn't have been able to rely upon them. I suspected the Guardians of the Blood (weird humans who lived inside Vampire Mountain and donated their blood in exchange for the internal organs of dead vampires) of being part of the conspiracy, but I'd thought Kurda was the only vampire traitor — it looked like I was wrong.

If Mr Crepsley and Arra hadn't been concentrating so hard on the search, they'd have realized something was amiss — the sword-bearing vampires were edgy, all nervous glances and itchy fingers. I'd love to have jumped out and shocked Kurda — he was the edgiest of the lot — but common sense prevailed. If I was spotted alive, he and his men would kill me and the three true vampires. As long as they believed I was dead, they wouldn't do anything to give themselves away.

I spent a long time studying the faces of Kurda's

companions, committing them to memory. I wondered how many more were in on the plot to destroy the clan. Not many, I bet. The vampires with him were very young. Kurda most likely recruited them himself and talked them round to his way of thinking before they learnt the ways of the vampires. More experienced vampires, who valued honour and loyalty, would never dream of being in league with a traitor.

After a while, the group came to a halt in a small clearing, where they sat and rested, except Mr Crepsley, who spent the period anxiously pacing. I tapped Streak's shoulder, then pointed towards the clearing — I wanted to get closer. The wolf hesitated, sniffed the air, then led the way forward. We carefully crawled to within seven or eight metres of the clearing, where we stopped, hidden by a dead tree trunk. With my developed sense of hearing, I could eavesdrop perfectly from here.

Nothing was said for a number of minutes. The vampires were blowing into their cupped hands and tugging their jackets closer about themselves, shivering from the cold. I smiled as I thought how uncomfortable they'd feel if they were in my compromising position.

After a while, Kurda got up and walked over to Mr Crepsley. "Think we'll find him?" the traitor asked, feigning concern.

Mr Crepsley sighed. "Probably not. But I would like to keep searching. I wish to locate his body and cremate him fittingly."

"He might still be alive," Kurda said.

Mr Crepsley laughed bleakly. "We traced his path through the tunnels. We know he fell into the stream and did not emerge. You truly think he may have survived?"

Kurda shook his head, as though deeply depressed. The dirty swine! He mightn't think I was alive, but he wasn't taking any chances either. If not for that sword of his, I'd have—

I calmed down and tuned back into the conversation. Arra had joined the pair and was talking. "...saw wolf tracks further back. They might have discovered his body and devoured him. We should check."

"I doubt if they would have eaten him," Mr Crepsley said. "Wolves respect vampires, as we respect them. Besides, his blood would have poisoned them and we would have heard their mad howling."

There was a brief moment of silence, then Arra muttered, "I'd love to know what happened in those tunnels. If Darren had been by himself and fallen in, I could understand it, but Gavner has disappeared too."

My insides froze at the mention of Gavner.

"Either he fell into the stream trying to save Darren," Kurda said lightly, "or Darren fell in trying to save him. That's the only answer I can think of."

"But how did they fall in?" Arra asked. "The stream wasn't wide where they fell. They should have been able to clear it. Even if it *was* too wide for them, why didn't they just jump where it was narrower? It makes no sense."

Kurda shrugged and pretended to be as baffled as the others.

"At least we know that Gavner is dead," Mr Crepsley remarked. "Although we have not found his body, the absence of his mental signal means he breathes no longer. His death distresses me, but the uncertainty regarding Darren unsettles me more. The odds are stacked against his being alive, but until we have proof that he is dead, I shall not be able to accept it."

It was oddly comforting to know that even in the midst of worry, Mr Crepsley had lost none of his elaborate ways of talking.

"We'll go on searching," Kurda said. "If he can be found, we'll find him."

Mr Crepsley shook his head and sighed again. "No," he said. "If we do not locate his body tonight, we must abandon the search. There is your investiture to prepare for."

"Forget the investiture," Kurda snorted.

"No," Mr Crepsley said. "The night after next, you become a Prince. That takes precedence above all else."

"But—" Kurda began.

"No," Mr Crepsley growled. "Your investiture as a Prince is more important than the loss of Gavner and Darren. You have bucked tradition already by leaving the confines of the mountain so close to the ceremony. You must stop thinking about Darren. As a Prince, it is your duty to put the will and wishes of others before your own. Your people expect you to spend tomorrow fasting and preparing for the investiture. You must not disappoint them."

"Very well," Kurda groaned. "But this isn't the end of it.

I'm as upset by what's happened as you are. I won't rest until we know for sure if Darren is alive or dead."

The hypocrite! Standing there, acting innocent, pretending to be upset. If only I'd had a gun or a crossbow, I'd have shot him dead where he stood, the laws of the vampires — which forbid the use of weapons such as guns and bows — be damned!

When the vampires moved on, I stayed where I was, thinking hard. Talk of Kurda's investiture had disturbed me. It had slipped my mind that he was due to be made a Vampire Prince. But now that I thought about it, things took ominous shape. I'd thought the vampaneze just meant to kill as many vampires as they could and take over the mountain, but the more I considered it, the less sense that made. Why go to all that risk just to take over a bunch of caves they couldn't have cared less about? And even if they killed every vampire present, there were plenty more who could hurry to the mountain and fight to reclaim it.

There must be a logical reason for them being here, and I thought I knew what it was — *the Stone of Blood*. The Stone of Blood was a magical stone with which a vampire or vampaneze could locate the whereabouts of almost every vampire on the face of the planet. With the Stone, the vampaneze could track down and destroy vampires at will.

The Stone was also rumoured to be the only object that could save the vampires from being obliterated by the legendary Lord of the Vampaneze, who was supposed to arise one night and lead the vampaneze into a victorious fight with the vampires. If the dreaded Lord was coming – as Mr Tiny said – the vampaneze would naturally be eager to get their hands on the one thing which stood between them and total victory!

But the Stone of Blood was magically protected in the Hall of Princes. No matter how many vampires the vampaneze killed, or how much of the mountain they claimed, they'd never be able to enter the Hall of Princes and get at the Stone of Blood, because only a Vampire Prince was capable of opening the doors to the Hall.

Only. A. Vampire. Prince.

Like Paris Skyle, Mika Ver Leth, Arrow, or Vancha March. Or – the night after next – *Kurda Smahlt.*

That was the plan! Once Kurda was invested, he'd be able to open the doors to the Hall of Princes whenever he liked. When he was ready, he'd sneak the vampaneze up from the caves and tunnels – he knew ways into the Halls which no one else knew – lead them to the Hall of Princes, kill everyone there, and take control of the Stone of Blood. Once that was in his hands, vampires everywhere would have to do what he said — or perish disobeying him.

In less than forty-eight hours Kurda would be invested and the Hall would be his for the taking. Nobody knew of his treachery, so nobody could stop him — except *me.* Reluctant as I was to face the vampires who'd condemned me to death, it was time to return to Vampire Mountain. I had to warn the Generals and Princes before Kurda could betray them. Even if they killed me for it…

CHAPTER NINE

ONCE WE were back with the pack, I told Streak I had to leave for Vampire Mountain. The wolf growled and loosely grabbed my right ankle with his fangs, trying to keep me with him. "I have to go!" I snapped. "I must stop the vampaneze!"

Streak released me when I mentioned the vampaneze, snarling softly. "They plan to attack the vampires," I said quietly. "They'll kill them all unless I stop them."

Streak stared at me, panting heavily, then pawed the snow, sniffed the marks he'd made, and yelped. It was obvious he was trying to communicate something important to me, but I couldn't interpret his actions. "I don't understand," I said.

Streak growled, again ran his nose over the tracks he'd made, then turned and padded away. I followed wonderingly. He led me to a shabby she-wolf resting slightly away from the pack. I'd noticed her before, but hadn't paid much attention to her — she was old, not far from death's door, and hadn't much to do with the pack, surviving off scraps they left behind.

The she-wolf regarded us suspiciously as we approached. Struggling to her feet, she backed away cautiously, but Streak dropped to his belly and rolled over to show he meant no harm. I did the same and the she-wolf relaxed. When Streak sat up, he pressed close to the she-wolf, whose eyes weren't strong, and stared at her long and hard, growling softly, meaningfully. He made marks in the snow, similar to the ones he'd made for me, then barked at the old she-wolf. She peered at the marks, then up at me, and whined. Streak barked again, to which she replied with a louder, sharper whine.

As I studied the wolves, wondering what was going on, it suddenly struck me that Streak was asking the old she-wolf – I decided on an impulse to call her Magda (my grandmother's name) – to lead me to Vampire Mountain. But all the wolves knew where the mountain was. Why was Streak asking this ancient, pitiful she-wolf to lead me? It made no sense. Unless… My eyes widened. *Unless* Magda knew a way not just *to* the mountain, but *up* it!

"You know how to get inside!" I gasped, crouching forward with excitement. Magda stared at me blankly, but I knew in my gut I was right. I could find my way up the mountain by myself, using common, marked passages, except it would be very difficult to avoid detection that way. But if Magda knew of older, less-used passages, I might be able to sneak in!

I turned to Streak imploringly. "Can she take me there? *Will* she?"

Streak ignored me and butted Magda softly with his head, scratching at the marks he'd made in the snow. The she-wolf whined one last time, then lowered her head obediently. I wasn't happy that Streak had bullied her into obeying him, but my need to get safely to the Princes at the top of Vampire Mountain was paramount — if a bit of bullying was required to help me sneak past the vampaneze, so be it.

"How far up the mountain can she take me?" I asked. "To the top, the Hall of Princes?" But this was too much for the wolves to comprehend — I'd just have to let her lead me as far as she could, and make my own way from there.

"Can we go now?" I asked, eager to be under way — I wasn't sure how long the trek would take, and time was precious.

Magda struggled to her feet, ready to follow me, but Streak snarled at me, then jerked his head at Magda and led her through the pack to feast on fresh meat — he wanted to feed her up before we set off, which was a wise move, given the sorry state she was in.

While Magda fed, I hopped nervously from foot to foot, thinking about the journey ahead and if we'd make it in time; if Magda really knew the way into and up the mountain; and even if I made it to the top, past the vampaneze, how exactly I could contact the Princes, before some over-anxious guard or co-conspirator of Kurda's saw me and hacked me down.

When Magda had eaten her fill, we set off. Streak accompanied us, along with two other young male wolves —

they seemed to be tagging along for the adventure! Rudi followed us out of camp, yapping with excitement, until Streak nipped him sharply and sent him scampering away. I'd miss the young cub, but there was no place for him where we were headed, so I bid him a silent farewell and left him behind, along with the rest of the pack.

The going was good at first. Wolves can't run especially fast but are incredibly resilient, able to maintain a steady pace for hours on end. We surged through the forest, across snow and rocks, making great time.

Then Magda tired. The she-wolf wasn't used to matching the pace of young, tireless males, and wilted. The wolves would have run on ahead, leaving her to catch up later, but I didn't like the idea of abandoning her. When they saw me slow down to jog along beside her, they checked and circled back to join us.

We rested for a few minutes every hour or so. As day dawned and developed, I began to recognize my surroundings. By my reckoning, allowing for our pace and pauses, we should reach the tunnels a couple of hours before sunset.

It actually took a little longer than I thought. When the ground rose, Magda's pace slowed even further. We still made the tunnels an hour before the sun went down, but I was filled with pessimism — Magda was in very poor shape. If the route to the tunnels had left her panting for breath and shaking with exhaustion, how would she cope with a long, testing climb up the mountain?

I said to Magda that she could stay here and leave me to make my own way, but she growled stubbornly. I got the sense that she intended to press ahead, not for my sake — but her own. Old wolves were seldom given the opportunity to shine. Magda was relishing her role and would rather die on the climb than quit. As a half-vampire, I understood that, so even though I wasn't pleased about letting the she-wolf exhaust herself on my account, I decided not to deter her.

We spent the night waiting in the tunnel near the base of the mountain. The young wolves were restless and eager to proceed, but I knew that night was when the vampires and vampaneze would be most active, so I held my position and the wolves had no choice but to stay with me. Finally, as the sun rose on the land outside, I stood and nodded, and we climbed.

The tunnels Magda led us through were mostly narrow and unused. Many were natural tunnels, as opposed to the mainly vampire-carved tunnels which linked the Halls. A lot of crawling and slinking along on our bellies was required. It was uncomfortable (and painful in places for someone without any clothes!) but I didn't mind — since no vampires or vampaneze used these tunnels, nobody could catch me!

We stopped for regular rest periods. The climb was having a dreadful effect on Magda – she looked ready to topple over and die – but she wasn't the only one who found the going tough. All of us were sweating and panting, groaning from aching muscles and bones.

While we rested in a cave that was faintly lit by luminous lichen, I fell to wondering how Magda knew about these tunnels. I guessed she must have wandered in here when she was younger – perhaps lost, starving, separated from her pack – and found her way up through trial and error, to safety, warmth and food. If that was the case, she had a truly incredible memory. I was marvelling at this – and at the memories of animals in general – when Streak's nose lifted sharply. He sniffed the air, then got to his paws and padded to the mouth of the tunnel leading out of the cave. The younger wolves joined him, and all three bared their fangs and growled softly.

I was instantly alert. Picking up a sharp stone, I rose to investigate the cause of their concern. But as I was crossing the cave, focusing on the wolves, a slim figure dropped suddenly and silently from the shadows overhead, knocked me to the ground, and roughly jammed a large bone between my lips, choking me and cutting short my panicked cry!

CHAPTER TEN

As I raised my hands to fight, the three male wolves began to bark — but not at me or my assailant. They were focused on some other danger, further up the tunnel, and took no notice of the trouble I was in. Nor did Magda, who lay peacefully where she was and gazed at me with a curious but unalarmed expression.

Before I could strike, the person holding me said something that sounded like "Gurlabashta!" I tried to shout in response, but could manage only a muffled grunt because of the bone jammed between my teeth. "Gurlabashta!" my attacker snapped again, then eased the bone out and pressed a couple of dry fingers to my lips.

Realizing my life wasn't under threat, I relaxed and suspiciously studied the person who'd knocked me to the floor. With a start, I saw that it was one of the pale-skinned, white-eyed Guardians of the Blood. He was a thin, anxious-looking man. Putting a finger to his own lips, he pointed at the wolves — barking louder than ever — then up at the roof of the cave, where he'd dropped from. Pushing me over to the wall, he pointed out fingerholds in the rocks, then scrambled up into darkness. I lingered doubtfully a moment, then glanced at the agitated wolves and followed him up.

There was a crevice at the top of the wall, which the Guardian guided me into. He slid into a small hole close by. I waited in silence, my heart beating loudly. Then I heard a voice addressing the angry wolves. "Quiet!" someone hissed. "Shut up, you mangy curs!"

The wolves quit howling, but continued growling menacingly. They backed away from the tunnel mouth, and moments later I saw a purple-skinned face poke out of the shadows — a vampaneze!

"Wolves!" the vampaneze snarled, spitting on the ground. "Curse their eyes!"

"Leave them be," a second vampaneze said behind him. "They won't interfere with us if we keep out of their way. They're just scavenging for food."

"If they keep yapping, they could bring the vampires down on us," the first vampaneze murmured ominously, and I saw the blade of a sharp knife glint by his side.

"They're only barking because of us," his companion said, dragging him away. "They'll stop once we..."

Their voices faded and I heard no more of them after that.

When I was sure the way was clear, I looked over to where the Guardian of the Blood was hiding, to thank him for his unexpected assistance — but he wasn't there. He must have slipped away while I wasn't looking. I shook my head with confusion. I'd thought the Guardians were in league with the vampaneze, since one of them ignored my cries for help when I was fleeing from Kurda and his allies, and left me to them. Why help me now when they'd abandoned me then?

Mulling it over, I climbed down and rejoined the wolves. They were still sniffing the air guardedly, but had stopped growling. After a while, we followed Magda out of the cave as she resumed her way and led us further up the mountain. She slinked ahead even slower than before, though I didn't know if this was because of exhaustion or the threat of the vampaneze.

Some hours later, we reached the lower Halls at the top of the mountain, and skirted around them. We passed disturbingly close to the store-rooms at one stage. I could hear vampires at work behind the walls, getting ready for the large feast which would follow Kurda's investiture. I held my breath and listened for a few minutes but their words were muffled and I soon moved on, for fear one of them would discover us.

I kept expecting Magda to come to a stop, but she led us higher and higher, further up the mountain than I thought possible. I was beginning to think we must be almost at the very top when we came to a tunnel which cut upwards sharply. Magda studied the tunnel, then turned and gazed at me — I could tell by the expression in her eyes that she'd brought me as far as she could. As I dashed forward, eager to check where the tunnel led, Magda about-faced and limped away.

"Where are you going?" I called. The she-wolf paused and glanced back, tired resignation in her stare — she couldn't manage the climb. "Wait here and we'll collect you later," I told her. Magda snarled, pawed the ground and ruffled her fur — and I got the sense that she was going away to *die*. "No," I said softly. "If you just lie down and rest, I'm sure—"

Magda interrupted with a short shake of her head. Staring into her sad eyes, I began to comprehend that this was what she wanted. She'd known when she set out that the journey would prove too much for her. She'd chosen to undertake it all the same and die usefully, rather than struggle along after the pack for another season or two, perishing slowly and miserably. She was prepared for death, and welcomed it.

Crouching, I ran my hands over the tired she-wolf's head and gently rubbed the thin hairs on her ears. "Thank you," I said simply. Magda licked me, rubbed her nose against my left cheek, then hobbled away into darkness, to find a secluded spot where she could lie down and quietly leave this world behind.

I remained where I was a while, thinking about death and how the wolf had accepted it so calmly, remembering how I'd run when it had been my time to face it. Then, shrugging off such morbid thoughts, I entered the tunnel and climbed.

The wolves had a harder time on the final stretch than me. Even though they were great climbers, the rock was sheer, unsuited to sharp claws, and they kept slipping to the bottom. Finally, tired of hanging about, I slid down and let the wolves go ahead of me, using my head and shoulders to brace them when they lost their footing.

Several minutes later, we found ourselves on level ground, in a small, dark cave. The air here was musty, made worse by the strong stench of the hairy wolves. "You three wait here," I told them in a whisper, afraid their smell would carry to any nearby vampires. Shuffling forward, I came to a wall of thin, fragile rock. Dim light shone through several tiny holes and cracks. I pressed my eyes to the gaps but they were too small to see through. Inserting the nail of my right little finger into one of the larger cracks, I worked gently at the stone, which crumbled, widening the hole. Leaning forward, I was able to see through to the other side — and was astonished to find myself at the rear of the Hall of Princes!

Once I'd recovered from the shock — there was only supposed to be one way up to the Hall of Princes! — I began considering my next course of action. This had worked out far more neatly than I'd ever dared dream, and it was now up to me to make the most of my incredible good fortune. My first instinct was to burst through the thin wall and scream for the Princes, but the guards of the Hall or one of the traitors might cut me down dead if I did, killing my message with me.

Retreating from the wall, I returned to the wolves and led them back down the steep tunnel, where there was more space and air. Once comfortable, I lay down, closed my eyes, and fell to thinking about how to make contact with the Princes — while at the same time avoiding the spears and swords of the vicious traitors and well-meaning guards!

CHAPTER ELEVEN

I WISHED to speak to the Princes directly — but I couldn't just march up to the doors of the Hall and ask the guards to let me in! I could wait for one of the Princes to emerge and hail him, but they didn't leave the throne room very often. What if Kurda made his move before I could act? I thought about sneaking down to the doors and slipping in the next time they were open, but it was unlikely that I could evade the attention of the guards. Besides, if Kurda was inside and saw me, he might make an end of me before I had a chance to speak.

That was my greatest fear — that I'd be killed before I warned the Princes of the peril they faced. With this in mind, I decided it was essential that I contact somebody before approaching the Princes, so that if I died, my message wouldn't die with me.

But who to trust? Mr Crepsley or Harkat were the ideal choices, but there was no way I could make it to their cells undetected. Arra Sails and Vanez Blane also dwelt too deep within the mountain to be easily reached.

That left Seba Nile, the ancient quartermaster of Vampire Mountain. His cell was close to the store-rooms. It would be risky, but I felt I could get to him without being seen. But could I trust him? He and Kurda were close friends. He'd helped the traitor make maps of infrequently-used tunnels, maps which the vampaneze might be using at this very minute to advance on the Hall of Princes. Was it possible that he was one of Kurda's allies?

Almost as soon as I raised the question, I knew it was ridiculous. Seba was an old-fashioned vampire, who believed in loyalty and the ways of the vampires above all else. And he'd been Mr Crepsley's mentor. If I couldn't trust Seba, I couldn't trust anybody.

I rose to go in search of Seba, and the wolves rose with me. Crouching, I told them to stay. Streak shook his head, growling, but I was firm with him. "Stay!" I commanded. "Wait for me. If I don't come back, return to the pack. This isn't your fight. There's nothing you can do."

I wasn't sure if Streak understood all that, but he squatted on his haunches and remained with the other wolves, panting heavily as he watched me leave, his dark eyes fixed on me until I vanished round a bend.

Retracing the path by which we'd come, I climbed back down the mountain. It didn't take long to reach the store-rooms. They were quiet when I arrived, but I entered cautiously, taking no chances, through the hole which Kurda had revealed to me during the course of my escape.

Finding nobody within, I started for the door leading to the tunnels, then stopped and glanced down at myself. I'd grown so used to being without clothes, I'd forgotten how odd I'd look to non-animal eyes. If I turned up in Seba's quarters like this, naked, dirty and wild, he might think I was a ghost!

There were no spare clothes in this room, so I ripped apart an old sack and tied a strip of it around my waist. It wasn't much of an improvement but it would have to do. I tied another few strips around my feet, so that I could pad more stealthily, then opened a sack of flour and rubbed a few handfuls of the white powder over my body, hopefully to mask the worst of my wolfish smell. When I was ready, I opened the door and crept into the tunnel beyond.

Though it would normally have taken no more than two or three minutes to get to Seba's rooms, I spent nearly four times that getting there, checking each stretch of tunnel several times before venturing down it, making sure I had somewhere to hide if vampires emerged unexpectedly.

When I finally reached the old quartermaster's door, I was shaking with anxiety, and stood in silence a few seconds, collecting myself. When I'd recovered, I knocked lightly. "Come in," Seba called. I entered. The quartermaster was standing by a chest with his back to me. "Over here, Thomas," he muttered, examining the insides of the chest. "I told you not to bother knocking. The investiture is a mere two hours away. We do not have time for–"

Turning, he saw me, and his jaw literally dropped.

"Hello, Seba," I smiled nervously.

Seba blinked, shook his head, blinked again. "*Darren?*" he gasped.

"The one and only," I grinned.

Seba lowered the lid of the chest and sat upon it heavily. "Are you a vision?" he wheezed.

"Do I look like one?"

"Yes," he said.

I laughed and advanced. "I'm no vision, Seba. It's me. I'm real." I stopped in front of him. "Feel me if you don't believe me."

Seba reached out a trembling finger and touched my left arm. When he realized I was solid, he beamed and rose. Then his face fell and he sat again. "You were sentenced to death," he said dolefully.

"I figured as much," I nodded.

"You fled."

"It was a mistake. I'm sorry."

"We thought you drowned. Your trail led to the stream and ended abruptly. How did you get out?"

"I swam," I said lightly.

"Swam where?" he asked.

"Down the stream."

"You mean … all the way … through the mountain? That is impossible!"

"Improbable," I corrected him. "Not impossible. I wouldn't be here if it was."

"And Gavner?" he asked hopefully. "Is he alive too?"

I shook my head sadly. "Gavner's dead. He was murdered."

"I thought so," Seba sighed. "But when I saw *you*, I—" He stopped and frowned. "*Murdered?*" he rumbled.

"You'd better stay sitting," I said, then proceeded to tell him the bare bones of my encounter with the vampaneze, Kurda's treachery, and what happened after.

Seba was shaking with rage when I finished. "Never did I think a vampire would turn against his brothers," he growled. "And one so highly respected! It sickens and shames me. To think I have drunk blood to that sham of a vampire's good health, and prayed to the gods to grant him luck! Charna's guts!"

"You believe me?" I asked, relieved.

"I might not recognize treachery when it is skilfully concealed," he said, "but I know the truth when it is revealed. I believe you. The Princes will too." Rising, he strode for the door. "We must hurry to warn them. The sooner we—" He paused. "No. The Princes will see no one until the time of investiture. They reside within their Hall and will not open the doors until twilight, when Kurda presents himself. That is the way it has always been. I would be turned away if I went there now."

"But you'll be able to get to them in time?" I asked anxiously.

He nodded. "There is a lengthy ceremony before the investiture. I will have plenty of time to interrupt and level these grievous charges against our supposed ally, Kurda Smahlt." The vampire was seething with rage. "Come to think of it," he said, eyes narrowing, "he is alone in his chambers now. I could go and slit the villain's throat before—"

"No," I said quickly. "The Princes will want to question him. We don't know who else is working with him, or why he did it."

"You are right," he sighed, shoulders slumping. "Besides, killing him would be a mercy. He deserves to suffer for what he did to Gavner."

"That's not the only reason why I don't want you to kill him," I said hesitantly. Seba stared at me and waited for me to continue. "I want to blow the whistle on him. I was with Gavner when he died. He was down in the tunnels because of me. I want to look into Kurda's eyes when I expose him."

"To show him how much you hate him?" Seba asked.

"No," I said. "To show him how much pain he's caused." There were tears in my eyes. "I hate him, Seba, but I still think of him as a friend. He saved my life. I'd be dead now if he hadn't intervened. I want him to know how much he's hurt me. Maybe it doesn't make sense, but I want him to see that I don't get any pleasure out of exposing him as a traitor."

Seba nodded slowly. "It makes sense," he said, stroking his chin and considering the proposal. "But it is dangerous. I do not think the guards will kill you, but one of Kurda's allies might."

"I'll take that chance," I said. "What do I have to lose? I'll be killed afterwards anyway, because I failed the Trials. I'd rather die on my feet, thwarting Kurda, than in the Hall of Death."

Seba smiled warmly. "You are a true, courageous vampire, Darren Shan," he said.

"No," I replied softly. "I'm just trying to do the right thing, to make up for running away earlier."

"Larten will be proud of you," Seba remarked.

I couldn't think of anything to say to that, so I just blushed and shrugged. Then we sat down together and discussed various plans for the climactic night ahead.

CHAPTER TWELVE

I DIDN'T really want to involve the wolves any further – in case they were killed – but they remained seated, panting patiently, when I tried chasing them off. "Go!" I hissed, slapping their flanks. "Home!" But they weren't dogs and they didn't obey. I saw they planned to stick by me – the younger wolves even looked like they were relishing the thought of a fight! – so I gave up trying to drive them to safety, and instead settled back to wait for nightfall, judging the time by my internal body clock.

As the day was drawing to a close, we crawled back up the steep tunnel and made our way to the wall at the rear of the Hall of Princes. I set to work on the soft layer of rock and carefully carved out a gap big enough for us to squeeze through. I was surprised nobody had ever found this weak point before, but it was quite high up and from the other side the wall must have looked solid.

I paused briefly to consider the extraordinary run of luck I was enjoying. Surviving the gushing madness of the mountain stream; Rudi and Streak finding me when I was at my weakest; Magda leading me through the tunnels to the Hall of Princes. Even failing the Trials had been in one respect fortunate — I'd never have found out about the vampaneze if I hadn't come a cropper against the Blooded Boars.

Was it really just the luck of the vampires, or was it something more — like *destiny*? I'd never believed in preordained fate, but I was beginning to have my doubts!

Sounds of the approaching procession distracted me from my heavy thoughts. The hour of Kurda's investiture was upon us. It was time to act. Wriggling through the hole, I dropped to the floor, turned and caught the wolves as they slithered down. When we were all ready, we flattened close to the wall of the Hall and edged forward.

As we slipped around the curve of the dome, I saw the Generals who'd lined up to welcome Kurda Smahlt. They'd formed a guard of honour, stretching from the tunnel to the doors of the Hall. Almost all were armed, as were the rest of the vampires — the ceremony of investiture was the one time vampires could carry weapons into the chamber. Any one of the armed vampires could be a traitor, with orders to kill me on sight. I tried not to dwell on that horrible thought, for fear it might deter me.

The three Princes stood by the open doors of the dome, regally attired, waiting to blood Kurda and make him one of their own. I spotted Mr Crepsley and Seba close to the Princes. Mr Crepsley was staring in the direction of the tunnel – along with everybody else – but Seba had an eye out for me. When he caught sight of me, he nodded slightly. That meant he'd had words with a few of his staff and had positioned them nearby, with orders to stop any vampire who raised a weapon during the ceremony. Seba hadn't told his assistants about me – we'd agreed it was best to keep my presence a secret – and I hoped they wouldn't hesitate when I made my move, affording one of Kurda's men the chance to kill me.

The head of the procession entered the cave. Six vampires preceded Kurda, walking slowly in pairs, carrying the clothes which Kurda would slip on once he'd been invested. Next came two deep-voiced vampires, loudly chanting poems and stories, praising the Princes and Kurda. There were more of the chanting vampires behind, and their hymn-like cries carried up the tunnel and echoed round the cave.

Behind the first eight vampires came the vampire of the moment, Kurda Smahlt, hoisted aloft on a small platform by four Generals, clad in a loose white robe, blond head bowed, eyes closed. I waited until he was halfway between the tunnel and the Princes, then stepped out from the wall, strode forward – the wolves close on my heels – and shouted as loud as I could, "*STOP!*"

All heads turned and the chanting ceased immediately. Hardly any of the vampires recognized me at first – all they saw was a dirty, half-naked boy, covered in flour – but as I got closer, the penny dropped and they gasped and exclaimed. "Darren!" Mr Crepsley roared with delight and started towards me, arms outstretched. I ignored my mentor and stayed focused on the rest of the vampires, alert to signs of retaliation.

The traitors didn't delay. Two vampires in green uniforms raised their spears when they saw me, while another pulled out a pair of knives and moved forward to intercept me. Seba's men reacted splendidly, ignored the confusion, and darted forward to apprehend the spear-wielding vampires. They dragged them to the ground before they could launch their weapons, disarmed them and held them down.

But nobody could get to the vampire with the knives — he was too far ahead of Seba's assistants. He broke through the ranks of guards, pushed Mr Crepsley out of the way, and raced towards me. He threw one of the knives, but I ducked out of its way with ease. Before he could throw the other or get close enough to stick it into me, the two young wolves launched themselves at him and knocked him to the floor. They bit and clawed at him, howling with excitement and fury. He shrieked and tried fighting them off, but they were too powerful.

One of the wolves sunk its teeth into the vampire's throat and made a brutal end of him. I didn't mind — I was only concerned about not harming innocent vampires, and by the speed with which this one had reacted, and the determination he'd shown to kill me, he was without doubt one of Kurda's accomplices.

The other vampires in the cave had frozen with shock. Even Mr Crepsley stopped where he was, eyes wide, panting uncertainly. "Darren?" he asked shakily. "What is going on? How did—"

"Not now!" I snapped authoritatively, eyes peeled for traitors. There didn't appear to be any more, but I wasn't taking things for granted, not until I'd said my piece. "I'll tell you about it later," I promised Mr Crepsley, then calmly walked past him to face Kurda and the Princes. Streak padded along by my side, watching out for me, growling warningly.

Kurda had opened his eyes and raised his head at the start of the commotion, but had made no attempt to flee the platform or the cave. He stared at me with hard-to-read eyes as I advanced, more wistful than panicky, then rubbed the three small scars on his left cheek (made by the vampaneze when he was discussing peace terms with them some years before), and sighed.

"What's going on?" Mika Ver Leth roared, his expression as black as the clothes he wore. "Why are those vampires fighting? Break them apart immediately!"

"Sire!" Seba said quickly, before the order could be obeyed. "Those who raised weapons against Darren are not our allies. Those who hold them down do so at my command. I would strongly advise against releasing them until you have heard Darren out."

Mika stared hard at the calm old quartermaster. "You're part of this chaos, Seba?" he asked.

"I am, Sire," Seba said, "and proud to be."

"That boy fled from the judgement of the Princes," Arrow growled, the veins in his bald head throbbing thickly. "He is not welcome here."

"He will be, Sire, when you learn why he has come," Seba insisted.

"This is most objectionable," Paris Skyle said. "Never before has anyone interrupted the investiture of a Prince. I do not know why you are siding with the boy, but I think the two of you should be removed from the Hall until later, when we can—"

"No!" I shouted, pushing through the ranks of guards to stand directly before the Princes. Locking gazes with them, I growled so that all could hear: "You say nobody has ever interrupted the investiture of a Prince, and this might be true. But I say no one has ever sought to invest a *traitor* before, so it's time that—"

The cave erupted with furious roars. The vampires were incensed that I'd called Kurda a traitor (even those who hadn't voted for his investiture), and before I could make any moves to protect myself, a horde surged around me and started kicking, punching and tearing at me. The three wolves tried dashing to my rescue but were easily propelled by the sheer mass of vampires.

"Stop this!" the Princes roared. "Stop! Stop! Stop!"

Finally, the commands of the Princes seeped through, and those who'd surrounded me released me and shuffled backwards, eyes aflame with anger, muttering darkly. They hadn't hurt me — the press had been too tight for any of them to get in a decent blow.

"This is a grim night," Mika Ver Leth grumbled. "It's bad enough that a boy violates our laws and customs, but when fully-blooded vampires who should know better behave like a pack of barbarians in the presence of their Princes…" He shook his head, disgusted.

"But he called Kurda a traitor!" someone yelled out, and tempers flared again, as vampires hurled curses at me.

"Enough!" Mika bellowed. When silence had fallen, he fixed his gaze on me. He looked only slightly less enraged than those who'd attacked me. "Were it up to me," he snarled, "I'd have you bound and gagged before you could say another word. Then I'd see you hauled off to the Hall of Death, where you'd suffer the fate you deserve."

He paused and glared around at the vampires, who were nodding and murmuring approvingly. Then his eyes alighted on Seba and he frowned. "But one we all know, trust and admire has spoken up on your behalf. I have no respect for half-vampires who flee instead of standing to face their punishment, but Seba Nile says we should pay attention to what you have to say, and I for one am loath to disregard him."

"I agree with that," Paris Skyle grunted.

Arrow looked troubled. "I also respect Seba," he said, "but such a breach of decorum is deplorable. I think…" Looking hard at Seba, he changed his mind and nodded gruffly. "Very well. I'll side with Paris and Mika. But only for Seba's sake."

Turning to me, looking as kindly as he could given the circumstances, Paris said, "Say your piece, Darren — but make it quick."

"OK," I agreed, glancing up at Kurda, who was staring at me wordlessly. "Let's see if this is quick enough for you — Kurda Smahlt killed Gavner Purl." The vampires gasped, and looks of hatred were replaced with frowns of uncertainty. "At this very moment, dozens of vampaneze lurk in the tunnels beneath us, waiting to attack," I continued. Stunned silence greeted my words. "They were invited here by *him!*" I pointed at Kurda, and this time no voices were raised in anger. "He's a traitor," I whispered, and as all eyes locked on Kurda, mine dropped and a couple of confused tears rolled down my cheeks and fell to the dusty cavern floor.

CHAPTER THIRTEEN

A LENGTHY silence followed my accusations. Nobody knew what to say or think. If Kurda had vehemently denied the claims made against him, perhaps the Generals would have rallied to his side. But he just stood there, downcast, suffering their questioning stares without reply.

Finally, Paris Skyle cleared his throat. "These are grave charges to bring against any vampire," he said. "To level them at a Prince-to-be while he stands on the point of investiture…" He shook his head. "You understand what the consequences will be if you are lying?"

"Why would I lie?" I retorted. Turning, I faced the ranks of vampires. "Everyone knows I failed my Trials of Initiation and fled before I could be killed. By returning, I've condemned myself to execution. Do you think I'd do that for no good reason?" Nobody answered. "Kurda betrayed you! He's in league with the vampaneze. As near as

I can figure, he plans letting them into the Hall of Princes once he's been invested, to seize control of the Stone of Blood."

There were cries of astonishment at that.

"How do you know this?" Arrow yelled over the noise. The bald prince hated the vampaneze more than most, because one of them had killed his wife many years ago.

"I'm only guessing about the Stone of Blood," I replied, "but I've seen the vampaneze. Gavner saw them too. That's why Kurda murdered him. He'd have spared *my* life, but I threw myself into the stream in the Hall of Final Voyage. I was sure I'd die, but I survived. Once I'd recovered, I came back here to warn you."

"How many vampaneze are down there?" Arrow asked, eyes blazing.

"At least thirty — possibly more."

The three Princes glanced at each other uneasily.

"This makes no sense," Mika muttered.

"I agree," Arrow said. "But a lie this outlandish would be simple to disprove. If he wished to fool us, he would have chosen a less fantastic story."

"Besides," Paris sighed, "look in the boy's eyes — there is nothing but truth in them."

A roar disrupted the conversation. One of Kurda's accomplices had broken free and grabbed a knife from a General. Before he could get away, the guards closed ranks and encircled him. He pulled out a knife and prepared to fight to the death.

"No, Cyrus!" Kurda bellowed, his first words since I'd disrupted the procession. The vampire's hand dropped and he looked to Kurda for guidance. "It's over," Kurda said softly. "Don't spill blood unnecessarily. That was never our aim."

The vampire called Cyrus nodded obediently. Then, before the circle of guards could close on him, he put the tip of the knife to his heart and made a swift, fatal stab. As the dead traitor fell to the floor, all eyes turned once again to Kurda, and this time the faces of the vampires were grim.

"What have you to say in rebuttal of Darren's claims?" Mika asked, his voice thick with emotion.

"At this moment — nothing," Kurda responded coolly.

"You don't deny the charge?" Arrow shouted.

"I do not," Kurda said.

A horrified moan swept through the cave at Kurda's admission of guilt.

"Let's kill him *now!*" Arrow growled, to a huge cheer of approval.

"With respect, Sires," Seba interceded, "would it not make more sense to focus on the vampaneze before we execute our own? Kurda can wait — we should deal with the intruders first."

"Seba is right," Paris said. "The vampaneze must be put to the sword. There will be time for traitors later."

Turning to a handful of guards, he told them to take Kurda and the other traitor away and hold them captive. "And under no circumstances let them take their own lives," he warned. "That would be the easy way out. Keep them alive until we have time to interrogate them."

Beckoning me forward, he addressed the massed vampires. "We will retire to the Hall of Princes with Darren. I ask the rest of you to remain here while we discuss the ramifications of this horrific turn of events. When we have decided on an immediate course of action, we shall inform you. There will be open talks later, when the present danger has been dealt with."

"And see that no one leaves the cave," Mika barked. "We don't know how deep this conspiracy runs. I don't want word of this reaching the ears of those who stand opposed to the welfare of our clan."

With that, the four of us entered the Hall of Princes, followed by several of the more senior Generals, as well as Seba, Arra Sails and Mr Crepsley.

Some of the tension seeped out of the air when the doors closed behind us. Paris hurried off to check on the Stone of Blood, while Mika and Arrow trudged disconsolately to their thrones. Seba thrust some clothes into my hands and told me to slip them on. I did so quickly, then let the quartermaster lead me forward to converse with the Princes. I still hadn't had a chance to have a word with Mr Crepsley, though I smiled at him to show that I was thinking about him.

I started by telling the Princes about my flight through the tunnels with Kurda, Gavner coming after us, changing direction, running into the vampaneze, Gavner making his stand, and Kurda's betrayal. When I got to the part about the stream, Paris clapped his hands loudly and grinned.

"I never would have credited it," the one-eared Prince

chuckled admiringly. "Young vampires over-eager to prove themselves used to go down it in barrels hundreds of years ago, but none ever tried—"

"Please, Paris," Mika complained. "Let's leave the reminiscences till later."

"Of course," Paris coughed meekly. "Do continue."

I told about washing up on a bank far away from Vampire Mountain, being found by the wolves and nursed back to health.

"That is not so extraordinary," Mr Crepsley interrupted. "Wolves have often given succour to abandoned children."

I described how I'd seen Mr Crepsley and Arra searching for me, but had kept my head down because of Kurda and the sword-wielding vampires.

"These two traitors," Mika said darkly. "Did you spot them in the cave?"

"Yes," I said. "They were two of the three who tried to kill me. The vampire stopped by the wolves was one. The other was captured and taken away with Kurda."

"I wonder how many more were part of this?" Mika mused.

"In my estimation — none," Paris said.

"You think there were only four of them?" Mika asked.

Paris nodded. "Vampires are not easily turned against their own. The three with Kurda were young and, if I remember correctly, all were blooded by him — the only three he ever blooded. Also, it is logical to assume that any in league with him would have been in the cave to witness his investiture. They would surely have acted along with the others to silence Darren before he could speak.

"I do not suggest we dismiss the possibility that there are one or two more we should be wary of," Paris concluded, "but it would be unhelpful to believe the rot is widespread. This is a time to pull together as one, not set in motion a series of unsettling witch hunts."

"I agree with Paris," Arrow said. "The suspicion must be stamped out before it has a chance to take hold. If we fail to re-establish trust swiftly, no vampire will be able to place faith in another, and anarchy will be rife."

I hurried through the rest of my story, bringing them up to date, telling them about Magda, my climb through the tunnels, how I contacted Seba to make sure word of Kurda's treachery wouldn't die with me if I was killed. I also mentioned the Guardians of the Blood, how one had failed to help when I cried out to him in the Hall of Final Voyage, but how another had come to rescue during my climb up the mountain.

"The Guardians of the Blood keep their own council," Seba said — he knew more about the Guardians than most. "They are loath to interfere directly in our affairs, which is why they would not have reported to us when they learned about the vampaneze. But indirect interference — such as hiding you when danger loomed — is permitted. Their neutrality is exasperating, but in keeping with their ways and customs. We should not hold it against them."

There was a long, thoughtful silence when I finished, broken eventually by Mika Ver Leth, who smiled wryly and said, "You put the clan's interests before your own. We cannot overlook your Trials of Initiation failure, or the fact that you ran from sentencing — but any dishonour you incurred has been cancelled out by this act of selfless dedication. You are a true vampire, Darren Shan, as worthy to walk the night as any I know."

I bowed my head to hide my shy smile.

"Enough of the praise," Arrow grunted. "There are vampaneze to kill. I won't rest until every last one has been hung over the stakes in the Hall of Death and dropped a dozen times. Let's storm down there and—"

"Easy, my friend," Paris said, laying a calming hand on the Prince's arm. "We must not rush into this. Our best trackers followed Darren's trail through the tunnels, passing close to the caves where the vampaneze were camped. Kurda would have thought of this and relocated them, so they would not be discovered. Our first priority must be to find them. Even after that, we must tread carefully, for fear they hear us coming and slip away."

"Very well," Arrow groaned. "But *I'm* leading the first wave against them!"

"I have no objection to that," Paris said. "Mika?"

"Arrow may lead the first wave," Mika agreed, "so long as I can lead the second, and he leaves enough for me to whet my blade on."

"It's a deal," Arrow laughed, the glint of battle lust in his eyes.

"So young and bloodthirsty," Paris sighed. "I suppose that means *I* have to stay behind and guard the Hall."

"One of us will relieve you before the end," Mika promised. "We'll let you mop up the stragglers."

"You are too kind," Paris grinned, then grew serious. "But that comes later. First, let us summon our best trackers. Darren will go with them to show them the inhabited caves. Once we—"

"Sires," Seba interrupted. "Darren has not eaten since leaving the pack of wolves, and has not partaken of human blood since departing Vampire Mountain. May I feed him before you send him off on so important a mission?"

"Of course," Paris said. "Take him to the Hall of Khledon Lurt and give him whatever he wants. We will send for him presently."

Though I'd have rather stayed and discussed the situation with the Princes, I was starving, and offered no protest as Seba led me away, through the cave of ogling vampires, down to the Hall of Khledon Lurt. In the Hall, I tucked into one of the most satisfying meals of my life, not forgetting to offer up a prayer of silent thanks to the gods of the vampires for helping me through my great ordeal — while asking them to guide all of us safely through the hardships still to come.

CHAPTER FOURTEEN

MR CREPSLEY brought Harkat to see me while I was eating. The Little Person hadn't been allowed to attend the Investiture – only vampires were permitted at the prestigious event – and knew nothing about my return until he walked into the Hall and spotted me shovelling food down my throat. "Darren!" he gasped, hurrying forward.

"'Lo, Harkat," I mumbled around a mouthful of fried rat.

"What are ... you doing ... here? Did they ... catch you?"

"Not exactly. I gave myself up."

"*Why?*"

"Don't ask me to explain it now," I pleaded. "I've just got through telling the Princes. You'll pick the story up soon enough. Tell me what's been happening while I was away."

"Nothing much," Harkat said. "The vampires were ...

furious when they … found out you'd fled. I told them … I knew … nothing about it. They didn't … believe me, but I … stuck to my … story, so there was … nothing they could … do."

"He would not even tell *me* the truth," Mr Crepsley said.

I looked at the vampire, ashamed of myself. "I'm sorry I ran away," I muttered.

"So you should be," he grunted. "It was not like you, Darren."

"I know," I moped. "I could blame Kurda – I wouldn't have run if he hadn't talked me into it – but the truth is I was scared and seized the opportunity to get away when it presented itself. It wasn't just dying that I was worried about — there was also the walk to that horrible Hall of Death, then being hung above the stakes and…" I shivered at the thought.

"Do not chastise yourself too much," Mr Crepsley said softly. "I am more to blame for letting them subject you to the Trials in the first place. I should have insisted upon a suitable period of time to prepare for the Trials and the consequences of failure. The fault is ours, not yours. You reacted as anyone who had not been fully versed in the ways of the vampires would have."

"I say it was fate," Seba murmured. "Had he not fled, we would never have been alerted to Kurda's treacherous nature or the presence of the vampaneze."

"The hands of … fate keep time … on a heart-shaped … watch," Harkat said, and we all turned to stare at him.

"What does that mean?" I asked.

He shrugged. "I'm not sure. It just … popped into my … head. It's something Mr … Tiny used to say."

We looked at each other uneasily, thinking about Mr Tiny and the heart-shaped watch he was so fond of playing with.

"You think Desmond Tiny could have had something to do with this?" Seba asked.

"I do not see how," Mr Crepsley said. "I believe Darren had the natural luck of the vampires on his side. On the other hand, where that dark horse Tiny is concerned — who knows?"

While we sat puzzling it over — the meddling fingers of fate, or sheer good fortune? — a messenger from the Princes arrived, and I was escorted through the lower Halls and tunnels to link up with the trackers and set off in search of the vampaneze.

Vanez Blane — who'd trained me for my Trials — was among the five chosen trackers. The one-eyed games master took my hands in his and squeezed hard by way of greeting. "I knew you would not desert us," he said. "Others cursed you, but I was sure you'd return once you had time to think things through. I told them it was a poor decision made in haste, which you'd shortly set right."

"I bet you didn't *bet* on me returning," I grinned.

"Now that you mention it — no, I didn't," he laughed. Vanez examined my feet to make sure my padding was adequate. All the trackers were wearing soft shoes. He offered to find a pair for me but I said I'd stick with the scraps of sack.

"We must proceed with utmost caution," he warned. "No sudden movements, no lights, and no talking. Communicate by hand signals. And take this." He gave me a long, sharp knife. "If you have to use it, don't hesitate."

"I won't," I swore, thinking about the knife which had savagely cut short the life of my friend, Gavner Purl.

Down we went, as silently as we could. I'm not sure I could have found the way back to the cave on my own — I hadn't been paying much attention to the route that night — but the trackers had followed the trail I'd left when they came looking for me and knew which way to go.

We crawled through the tunnel under the stream. It wasn't as frightening this time, not after all I'd been through since last I passed this way. As we stood, I pointed wordlessly to the tunnel which connected the small cave to the larger one. Two of the trackers advanced and checked on the cave beyond. I listened intently for sounds of a struggle but there weren't any. Moments later, one of the trackers returned and shook his head. The rest of us trailed after him into the bigger cave.

My insides tightened when I saw the cave was deserted. It looked as if it had been empty since the beginning of time. I had an ugly premonition that we'd be unable to find the vampaneze and I'd be called a liar. Vanez, sensing this, nudged me gently and winked. "It'll be OK," he mouthed, then joined the others, who were exploring the cave cautiously.

It didn't take the trackers long to uncover evidence of the vampaneze and allay my fears. One found a scrap of cloth, another a fragment from a broken bowl, another a small pool of spit where a vampaneze had cleared his throat. When they'd gathered enough evidence, we returned to the smaller cave, where we held a quiet conversation, safe in the knowledge that the roar of the stream would cover our voices.

"It was vampaneze all right," one of the trackers said. "A couple of dozen at least."

"They covered their tracks admirably," another grunted. "We only unearthed them because we knew what to look for. We'd never have noticed if we'd been giving the cave a quick once-over."

"Where do you think they are now?" I asked.

"Hard to say," Vanez mused, scratching the lid of his blind eye. "There aren't a lot of caves nearby where that many vampaneze could comfortably hole-up. But they may have split into smaller groups and scattered."

"I doubt it," one of the others remarked. "If I was in charge of that lot, I'd want everyone to stick close together, in case we were discovered. I think we'll find them bunched-up, possibly close to an exit point, ready to fight or flee *en masse*."

"Let's hope so," Vanez said. "It could take ages to locate them all if they've split up. Can you find your way back to the Halls?" he asked me.

"Yes," I said, "but I want to come with you."

He shook his head. "We brought you down to show us the cave. Now that you've done that, there's no place for you here. We can move quicker without you. Return to the Halls and tell the others what we found. We'll be back when we find the vampaneze."

Seba met me at the gate of entry and escorted me up to the Hall of Princes. Many Generals had filed in to discuss the emergency, but apart from those with special permission to run errands, none had been allowed to leave the cave around the Hall, so a lot stood or sat outside, waiting for news to trickle through.

Mr Crepsley and Harkat were inside. The vampire was talking with the Princes. Harkat was standing to one side, with Madam Octa's cage. He presented it to me when I joined him. "I thought ... you'd be glad ... to see her," he said.

I wasn't really, but I pretended I was. "Great, Harkat," I smiled. "Thanks for thinking of it. I missed her."

"Harkat has been taking good care of your spider," Seba said. "He offered to give her to me when you went missing, but I told him to hang on to her. I said one never knew what lay around the corner — I had a feeling you might be back."

"You may wind up with her yet," I said morosely. "I seem to have won back my honour, but there's still my failure in the Trials to account for."

"Surely they won't ... punish you for ... that now?" Harkat said.

I glanced at Seba's face — it was stern and he said nothing.

Vanez Blane returned a couple of hours later with good news — they'd discovered the whereabouts of the vampaneze.

"They're in a long, narrow cave, close to the exterior of the mountain," Vanez explained to the Princes, wasting no time on rituals or pleasantries. "There's one way in and one way out. The exit tunnel runs straight to the outside, so they can make a quick getaway if they have to."

"We'll position men outside to catch them if they do," Mika said.

"That will be difficult," Vanez sighed. "The ground is steep where the tunnel opens out, and I'm sure they'll have sentries posted. I doubt that we'll be able to sneak men up there. It will be better to take them inside if we can."

"You think we cannot?" Paris asked sharply, alerted by Vanez's worried tone.

"It won't be easy, however we go about it," Vanez said. "No matter how delicately we mask our approach, we won't be able to surprise them. Once they become aware of us closing in, they'll throw up a rear phalanx to delay us while the majority escape."

"What if we block the tunnel from the outside?" Arrow asked. "Create an avalanche or something. Then they'd have to stand and fight."

"That's a possibility," Vanez agreed, "but blocking the tunnel may prove awkward. Besides, that would alert them to our presence and intentions, and they'd have time to prepare for us. I'd rather spring a trap."

"You think they might best us in a fair fight?" Arrow snorted.

Vanez shook his head. "No. We couldn't get close enough

to make a full count, but I don't think there's more than forty vampaneze down there, probably less. I've no doubt that we'll beat them." The vampires cheered Vanez's claim. "It's not the winning that bothers me," he shouted over their excited clamours. "It's the losses we'll incur."

"Damn the losses!" Arrow growled. "We've spilt blood before, dispatching vampaneze — who here will hesitate to spill it again?" By the roars it was plain that nobody would.

"That's easy to say," Vanez sighed when the cheers had died down. "But if we barge in and take them on without some sort of a distraction, we're looking at the possible loss of thirty or forty vampires, maybe more. The vampaneze have nothing to lose and will fight to the bitter, bloody end. Do *you* want to take responsibility for those casualties, Arrow?"

Much of the vampires' joy abated at Vanez's words. Even the eager, vampaneze-hating Arrow looked hesitant. "You think we'll lose that many?" he asked quietly.

"We'd be *lucky* to just lose thirty or forty," Vanez replied bluntly. "They've picked their spot expertly. We won't be able to rush or overwhelm them. We'll have to advance a handful at a time, taking them on one-to-one. Our superior numbers will lead to eventual victory, but it won't be swift or easy. They'll hurt us — *badly*."

The Vampire Princes shared an uneasy look. "Those sort of figures are unacceptable," Paris stated bleakly.

"They *are* a bit on the high side," Mika reluctantly concurred.

"Is it possible to create a diversion?" Mr Crepsley asked, joining in the discussion. "Could we flood or smoke them out?"

"I've thought of that," Vanez said. "I don't see any way of pumping enough water down there to trouble them. Fire would be ideal, but the cave's well ventilated. The ceiling's high and full of tiny cracks and holes. We'd have to get inside the cave and light a huge bonfire to create enough smoke to bother them."

"Then it will have to be a full-frontal attack," Paris declared. "We will send in our best spearists first, who should eliminate many of them before we go hand to hand. Our losses should not be so great that way."

"They'll still be substantial," Vanez objected. "Spearists won't have much room to operate. They might take out the watchguards by the entrance, but after that…"

"What option do we have?" Arrow snapped. "Would you rather we went down with a white flag and discussed peace terms?"

"Don't bellow at me in that tone!" Vanez shouted. "I'm as anxious to get at them as any vampire here. But it will be a pyrrhic victory if we fight one-on-one."

Paris sighed. "If that is the only victory on offer, we must accept it."

In the short silence which followed, I asked Seba what a pyrrhic victory was. "That is when the price of winning is too high," he whispered. "If we defeat the vampaneze, but lose sixty or seventy of our own troops doing so, it will be a worthless victory. The first rule of warfare is never to weaken yourself irreparably whilst destroying your enemies."

"There *is* one alternative," Paris said hesitantly. "We could run them off. If we made a lot of noise approaching, I am sure they would scatter rather than face us. The vampaneze are not cowards, but nor are they fools. They will not stand and fight a battle they are sure to lose."

Angry mutters greeted this suggestion. Most vampires believed that would be dishonourable. The consensus was that they'd rather confront the vampaneze.

"It is not the most honourable of tactics," Paris shouted over the heated whispers. "But we could pursue and fight them on the outside. Many would escape, but we would capture and kill enough of them to teach them a harsh lesson."

"Paris has a point," Mika said, and the muttering ceased. "I don't like it, but if it's a choice between letting most go or sacrificing forty or fifty of our own..."

Heads began nodding, slowly, unhappily. Paris asked Arrow what he thought of the suggestion. "I think it stinks," he snarled. "The vampaneze aren't bound by our laws — they can flit once outside. We'd catch virtually none of them." Flitting was the super-quick speed vampires and vampaneze could run at. By tradition, vampires were not allowed to flit on the way to and from Vampire Mountain.

"Were I a General," Arrow went on, "I'd object most vehemently to letting them go. I'd rather fight and die than concede ground to the enemy in such a meek fashion." He sighed miserably. "But, as a Prince, I must put the welfare of our people before the stirrings of my heart. Unless somebody can think of a plan to distract the vampaneze and clear the way for an attack, I will agree to running them off."

When nobody spoke up, the Princes called their leading Generals forward and discussed the best way to drive off the vampaneze and where they should place their men on the outside. An air of disappointment hung heavily over the Hall and most vampires stood or sat with their heads bowed, disgusted.

"They don't like this," I whispered to Seba.

"Nor do I," he replied, "but pride must be checked in the face of such aggressive odds. We could not allow our men to perish in horrifying numbers, all for the sake of honour. Reason must be obeyed, no matter how galling it might be."

I was as upset as the rest of the vampires. I wanted revenge for Gavner Purl. There was no satisfaction in letting the vampaneze wriggle off the hook. I'd spoilt their plans to invade the Hall of Princes, but that wasn't enough. I could imagine the smirk on Kurda's face when he learnt of our diplomatic decision.

As I stood, pouting, a tiny insect flew into Madam Octa's cage and got trapped in a small web she'd spun in a corner. The spider reacted swiftly and advanced on the struggling captive, disposing of it presently. I watched, mildly interested, then stiffened as a crazy thought struck me.

Gazing at the feeding spider, I let my brain whirl wildly, and the plan formed within a matter of seconds. It was simple yet effective — the very best sort.

Standing on my tip-toes, I cleared my throat three times before I managed to attract Mr Crepsley's attention. "Yes, Darren?" he asked wearily.

"Excuse me," I called, "but I think I know how to distract the vampaneze."

All conversation ceased and every pair of eyes settled on me. I stepped forward unbidden, and spoke nervously. As I outlined my proposals, the vampires started to smile. By the time I finished, most were laughing outright and chortling gleefully at the wicked, cunning scheme.

Voting was brief and unanimous. My plan was put to the vampires and, as one, they roared their approval. Without any further ado, the Princes and Generals fell to organizing their attack forces, while Seba, Mr Crepsley and me slipped away to gather together our own army of troops and prepare for the first stage of what, in a war film, would probably have been called *Operation Arachnid!*

CHAPTER FIFTEEN

OUR FIRST stop was the cave of Ba'Halen's spiders, where Seba had taken me when I was suffering from burns after my Trial in the Hall of Flames. The quartermaster went in by himself, carrying Madam Octa in the palm of his left hand. He was grim-looking and empty handed when he emerged, eyes half-closed.

"Did it work?" I asked. "Were you able—"

He shushed me with a quick wave of a hand. Closing his eyes completely, he concentrated fiercely. Moments later, Madam Octa crept out of the cave, followed by a spider with light grey spots on its back. I recognized that spider — I'd seen it mooning after Madam Octa before.

Behind the grey-spotted spider came several more of the mildly poisonous mountain spiders. Others followed, and soon a thick stream of spiders was flowing out of the cave and gathering around us. Seba was directing them, communicating mentally with the wild, eight-legged predators.

"I am going to transfer control now," he told Mr Crepsley and me when all the spiders were in place. "Larten, take the spiders to my right. Darren, those to my left."

We nodded and faced the spiders. Mr Crepsley was able to communicate without the use of aids, as Seba was, but I needed my familiar flute to focus my thoughts and transmit them. Raising it to my lips, I blew a few practice notes. It was awkward, because of my bent right thumb – which still hadn't straightened out – but I quickly learnt to compensate for the damaged digit. Then I stood awaiting Seba's word.

"Now," he said softly.

Gently, I played and sent a repeated mental message to the spiders. "Stay where you are," I told them. "Hold, my beauties, hold."

The body of spiders swayed uncertainly when Seba stopped transmitting his thoughts, before fixing on mine and Mr Crepsley's. After a few confused seconds they clicked into sync with our brainwaves and resumed their solid shape.

"Excellent," Seba beamed, stepping forward, careful not to squash any of the spiders. "I will leave you with them and go find others. Escort these to the meeting point and wait for me. If any start to drift away, send Madam Octa to rally them — they will obey her."

We let Seba exit, then turned towards one another. "You need not play the flute continuously," Mr Crepsley advised. "A few whistles and commands once we get moving should be enough. They will fall into place behind us and advance naturally. Save the flute for stragglers or those of a rebellious nature."

"Should we lead or take the rear?" I asked, lowering my flute to wet my lips.

"Lead," Mr Crepsley said. "But keep an eye on them and be prepared to drop back if need be, ideally without interrupting the march of the others."

"I'll try," I said, then faced front and played.

Off I set, Mr Crepsley beside me, the spiders scuttling along behind. When we reached the larger tunnels, we moved further apart to form two separate files.

It wasn't as difficult to command the spiders as I'd feared. A few gave me problems – they fought with others or tried to edge away – but a quick intervention on the part of Madam Octa was enough to knock them back into shape. She was revelling in her role and even started patrolling the ranks of her own accord, without prompting. She'd have made a great General if she'd been a vampire!

Finally, we pulled into the large cave we'd established as our base. We arranged the spiders around us in a circle, then sat in the middle of them and waited for Seba.

He was leading an army of spiders almost half as large again as ours when he arrived. "Where'd you get them all?" I asked, as they encircled those already in the cave.

"The mountain is full of spiders," he said. "One simply needs to know where to look." He sat beside us and smiled. "Having said that, I have never in my life seen such a concentration in one place at one time. It is enough to unnerve even a hardened handler such as myself!"

"I feel that way too," Mr Crepsley agreed, then laughed. "If they have such an effect on *us*, what sort of terror will they provoke in the unsuspecting vampaneze?"

"That is what we shall shortly discover," Seba chuckled.

While we waited to be contacted by the Princes, Mr Crepsley took my flute from me and fiddled with it. When he handed it back, it no longer worked, and so couldn't alert the vampaneze. The fact that it had been muted didn't matter — the music itself made no difference to the spiders. I only used the flute out of habit, after years of performing with Madam Octa at the Cirque Du Freak.

After a long, uncomfortable wait, we spotted a platoon of vampires slipping by. Arrow shortly appeared and advanced to the edge of the eight-legged sea. He gazed uneasily around at the spiders and came no closer. He was gripping two heavy, sharp-tipped boomerangs, and had three more strapped to his waist. The boomerang was his weapon of choice. "We're ready," he whispered. "The vampaneze haven't left their cave. Our troops are in position. The sun shines brightly outside. It is time."

We nodded obediently and got to our feet.

"You know what to do?" Mr Crepsley asked me.

"I take my spiders out," I responded. "I get close to the mouth of the tunnel, taking care not to be seen. You and Seba will guide your spiders forward, using the tiny cracks and holes in the walls and roof of the cave. You'll hold them there until I make the first move. I'll send my spiders against the guards in the tunnel opening. When you hear the commotion, you'll order yours in — then the fun begins!"

"Allow us a decent amount of time to position our spiders," Seba instructed me. "They will be difficult to manoeuvre, since we cannot see where they are going. It will be a slow, painstaking process."

"I'm in no hurry," I said. "Will three hours be enough?"

"That should be plenty," Seba said, and Mr Crepsley agreed.

We wished each other luck, shook hands, then I summoned my troops – the smallest of the three clusters of spiders, since they'd have the least to do – and set off for the outside.

The sun shone wanly in a mostly cloudless sky, which was helpful — the vampaneze guards would keep well back from the mouth of the tunnel to avoid the deadly rays of light.

I emerged about forty metres up from the tunnel. I held my position until all my spiders were out in the open around me, then urged them forwards, slowly and carefully. We crept down the mountain until we were ten metres shy of the tunnel, sheltered by a large rock which jutted out of the mountain face, providing perfect cover. This was as close to the tunnel as I dared get.

Once in place, I lay down and watched the sun cross the sky. I'd been chosen for the external leg of the operation partly because it provided fewer problems than the pair working within the mountain would have to deal with, but also because I was immune to the sun. It was vital that we attack by day — the vampaneze would be loath to leave their sanctuary and face the sun — but the vampires would have been hampered by the solar giant as much as their foes. Only I could move about outside as freely as I pleased.

When slightly more than three hours had passed, I blew mutely on my flute and ordered the spiders to spread out wide, before advancing. Only the spiders moved forward — I stayed where I was, hidden by the rock. The spiders formed a ring around the mouth of the tunnel. From the outside they looked harmless, but when they entered the cave, they'd assume a different dimension — they'd look more numerous, and a lot more threatening. Cramped spaces have a way of magnifying one's fears. The vampaneze within would hopefully feel they were under siege, and panic accordingly.

A couple of minutes to make sure the ranks were orderly. Then I gave the signal to enter. They slipped in silently, covering not just the floor of the tunnel, but also the walls and roof. If everything went as planned, the vampaneze would think the tunnel was coming alive with spiders.

I was supposed to stay where I was, out of the way, but the temptation to sneak forward and observe the unfolding of my plan proved too great to resist. Lying flat on the rough face of the mountain, I slid down to the top of the tunnel and listened for the sounds of chaos within.

I could hear the heavy breathing of vampaneze, further back from the entrance than I'd expected. For a while, that was all I could hear, calm and regular. I was starting to wonder if maybe the spiders had slipped through cracks and deserted back to their natural habitat. Then one of the vampaneze grunted: "Hey! Is it my imagination, or are the walls moving?"

His colleagues laughed. "Don't be stu–" one began, then stopped. "What in the name of the gods…?" I heard him gasp.

"What's happening?" somebody shouted, alarmed. "What are they?"

"They look like spiders," one of his less-agitated comrades answered.

"There's millions of them!" a vampaneze whimpered.

"Are they poisonous?" another asked.

"Of course not," the unafraid vampaneze snorted. "They're just ordinary mountain spiders. They can't do any–"

Blowing hard on my flute, I sent the order to the spiders: "*Now!*"

Inside the tunnel, screams erupted.

"They're dropping!" someone howled.

"They're all over me! Get them off! Get them off! Get them–"

"Calm down!" the level-headed vampaneze yelled. "Just brush them off and – *ahhhhh!*" he screamed, as the spiders seized hold and sank their fangs in.

Individually, the spiders were harmless — their bites were only mildly irritating. But the simultaneous bites of hundreds of them… That was a different matter entirely!

As the vampaneze thrashed around the tunnel, slapping

and stamping at the spiders, screaming with pain and fear, I heard others advance from within the cave to see what was wrong. Darting into the tunnel, I crouched down low and ordered the spiders to surge on ahead. As they obeyed, panicking the newcomers and forcing them backwards, the cave behind echoed with the screams and writhing of the massed vampaneze, as Mr Crepsley and Seba's spiders slipped from the walls and roof and worked their fearsome charms.

The battle had truly begun.

CHAPTER SIXTEEN

I WASN'T supposed to join in the fighting, but the furore of the terrifed vampaneze excited me, and before I knew what I was doing, I'd sneaked forward to observe what was happening within the cave.

It was incredible to watch. Spiders covered the floor and walls and – most vitally – the rioting vampaneze. The purple-faced wretches were leaping around like cartoon figures, yelling and screeching, desperately trying to repel the attack. Some used swords and spears, which were no use against the tiny invaders, who easily ducked the wild blows and darted forward to sink their fangs into exposed patches of flesh. The vampaneze with the swords and spears were doing almost as much damage as the spiders. Lashing out blindly, they connected with their colleagues, wounding several, even killing a few.

Some of the wiser vampaneze were struggling to establish control, roaring at the others to form ranks against the spiders. But the pandemonium dwarfed their efforts. They were ignored, sometimes knocked out of the way when they tried to intervene.

In the midst of the panic, Streak and the two younger wolves bounded into the cave from the far entrance, yapping, howling and snarling as loudly as possible. I don't think anybody had invited the wolves along — they simply came of their own accord, eager to be part of the rout!

When the vampaneze saw the wolves coming, several turned and bolted for the exit. They'd had enough — even the lethal sunlight seemed a welcome prospect in comparison to this! I thought about standing aside and letting them pass, but the battle lust was strong in me and adrenaline was pumping through every cell of my body. I wanted to keep them here if I could, so that they might suffer along with the rest of their despicable tribe. At the time, revenge was all I could focus on. It was all that seemed to matter.

Looking around, I spotted a spear which one of the tunnel guards had dropped during the course of their hasty retreat. Picking it up, I wedged the end against a crack in the floor, then pointed the tip at the charging vampaneze. The lead vampaneze saw me and tried to veer out of the way of the spear, but those behind pushed him on unwillingly. Running on to the spear, he impaled himself without any help from me.

Standing, I roughly shoved the vampaneze off the spear, then bellowed at those behind him. They must have thought the way was blocked by a horde of savage vampires, because they immediately about-faced and retreated. I laughed triumphantly and started after them, meaning to add a few more scalps to my collection. Then I happened to glance at the vampaneze who'd run on to my spear, and came to a sickened halt.

He was young, his face only a light shade of purple. He was crying and making soft, whimpering noises. Unable to stop myself, I crouched beside him. "It ... hurts!" he gasped, clutching at the deep, wide hole in his belly. His hands were red and I knew his cause was hopeless.

"It's OK," I lied. "It's only a flesh wound. You'll be up on your—" Before I could say any more, he coughed. Blood pumped out of his mouth, a huge torrent of it. His eyes widened, then closed. He groaned softly, fell back, shuddered, then died.

I'd killed him.

The thought shook me to my very core. I'd never killed before. Even though I'd been looking forward to punishing the vampaneze for what they did to Gavner, it was only now that I considered the consequences of my actions. This vampaneze – this person – was dead. I had taken his life and could never restore it.

Maybe he deserved death. He might have been rotten to the core and in dire need of killing. Then again, maybe he'd been an ordinary guy, like me or any of the vampires, only here because he'd been following orders. Either way, deserving or not, who was I to decide? I didn't have the right to pass judgement on others and kill them. Yet I'd done it. Excited by the fear of the vampaneze, intent on revenge, letting my heart rule my head, I'd raised a weapon against this man and killed him.

I hated myself for what I'd done. I wanted to turn tail and run, get far away and pretend this never happened. I felt cheap, dirty, nasty. I tried consoling myself with the thought that I'd done the right thing, but how did one separate right from wrong where killing was concerned? I'm sure Kurda thought *he* was doing right when he stabbed Gavner. The vampaneze thought *they* were doing right when they drained people they fed upon. However I looked at it, I had the awful feeling that I was now no better than any other killer, one of a vicious, terrible, inhuman breed.

Only my sense of duty held me in place. I knew that vampires would be attacking any moment. It was my job to keep the spiders active until they did, so that the vampaneze couldn't regroup and meet the assault head on. If I deserted my post, vampires would perish in great numbers as well as the vampaneze. I had to concentrate on the bigger picture, regardless of how I felt inside.

Sticking my flute back between my lips, I played and urged the spiders to swarm over the vampaneze. The scene looked so different in light of the life I'd taken. I no longer enjoyed watching the vampaneze shriek and lash out blindly, or saw them as evil villains on the receiving end of their just desserts. Instead I saw warriors, terrified and humiliated, stranded far from their homes and allies, about to be ruthlessly slaughtered.

At the height of the hysteria, the vampires attacked, led by a bellowing Arrow, who tossed his sharp-edged boomerangs at the vampaneze, one after the other, drawing blood with each. Spearists were beside and behind him, and their hurled weapons caused much damage and claimed many lives.

As vampires poured into the cave, the spiders withdrew, urged to retreat by the unseen Mr Crepsley and Seba. I held my spiders in place a while longer, keeping the panic alive at this end of the cave.

Within less than a minute, the vampires had stormed the whole of the cave, those with swords and knives replacing the first wave of spearists. They hadn't come in great numbers – if too many had poured into the narrow chamber, they'd have got in each other's way – but the thirty who'd entered appeared far more in comparison with the stricken vampaneze. It seemed as though there were five vampires to every one of their foes.

Arrow was in the thick of the action, leading by example, as mercilessly efficient with his swords as he'd been with his boomerangs. Vanez Blane stood close by the Prince, knives flashing, backing him up. Alarmed as they were by the spiders and wolves, the vampaneze quickly realized where the real threat lay, and hurriedly backed away from the clinically murderous pair.

Arra Sails was also part of the initial assault. She was in her element, attacking the vampaneze with a short sword in one hand, a spiked chain in the other, laughing brutally as they fell beneath her. I'd have cheered her display a few minutes earlier, but now felt only dismay at the sheer joy she and the other vampires were taking in the destruction.

"This isn't right," I muttered to myself. Killing the vampaneze was one thing — it had to be done — but relishing their downfall was wrong. There was something deeply unsettling about seeing the vampires extract so much ghoulish satisfaction from the massacre.

Confused as I was, I decided I'd best wade in and lend a hand. The sooner we made an end of the vampaneze, the sooner I could turn my back on the horror. Taking a sharp dagger from the man I'd killed, I called off my spiders, then threw my flute away and stepped forward to join the press of battling vampires and vampaneze.

I kept to the edges of the fighting, jabbing at the feet or legs of vampaneze, distracting them, making it easier for the vampires they were facing to disarm and kill them. I took no pleasure from the success of my endeavours, only forged ahead, determined to help bring things to a quick conclusion.

I spotted Mr Crepsley and Seba Nile entering the cave, their red robes billowing behind them, eager to be part of the bloodshed. I didn't hold their eagerness to kill against them. I didn't hold it against any of the vampires. I just thought it was misplaced and unseemly.

The fighting intensified shortly after Mr Crepsley and Seba joined the fray. Only the toughest and most composed of the vampaneze had survived the first period of madness, and now they battled grimly to the finish, making their stands, some alone, some in pairs, taking as many vampires to the grave with them as they could.

I saw the first vampire casualties slump to the ground, bellies sliced open or heads bashed in, bleeding and sobbing, crying out loud with pain. On the floor, dying, covered in blood, they looked no different to the vampaneze.

As the front-runners of the second vampire wave trickled into the cave, Vanez slapped Arrow's back and told him to leave. "*Leave?*" the Prince snorted. "It's just getting interesting!"

"You've got to go," Vanez roared, dragging Arrow away from the fighting. "It's Mika's turn to blood his blade. Go back to the Hall of Princes and relieve Paris, as you promised. You've had your fair share of the killing. Don't be greedy."

Arrow left reluctantly. On his way, he passed Mika, and the two clapped each other on the back, as though one was a substitute replacing the other in a game of football.

"Not pleasant, is it?" Vanez grunted, pulling up beside me. He was sweating freely and paused to dry his hands on his tunic as the fighting raged around us.

"It's horrible," I muttered, gripping my knife before me like a cross.

"You shouldn't be here," Vanez said. "Larten wouldn't approve if he knew."

"I'm not doing it for fun," I told him.

Looking deep into my eyes, Vanez sighed. "So I see. You learn quickly, Darren."

"What do you mean?" I asked.

He gestured at the warring, whooping vampires. "They think this is great sport," he laughed bleakly. "They forget that the vampaneze were once our brothers, that by destroying them, we destroy a part of ourselves. Most vampires never realize how pointless and savage war truly is. You were smart enough to see the truth. Don't ever forget it."

A dying vampaneze stumbled towards us. His eyes had been cut out and he was moaning pitifully. Vanez caught him, lowered him to the floor, and finished him off quickly and mercifully. When he stood, his face was grim. "But, painful as war is," he said, "sometimes it can't be avoided. We didn't seek this confrontation. Remember that later, and don't hold our aggression against us. We were forced into this."

"I know," I sighed. "I just wish there'd been some other way to punish the vampaneze, short of tearing them to pieces."

"You should leave," Vanez suggested. "This is where the truly dirty work begins. Return to the Halls and drink yourself senseless."

"I might do that," I agreed and turned away, leaving Vanez and the others to round up the final stubborn vampaneze. As I was departing, I spotted a familiar face among the crowd — a vampaneze with a dark red birthmark on his left cheek. It took me a moment to recall his name — *Glalda*, the one who'd spoken with Kurda in the tunnel when Gavner was killed. He'd wanted to kill me as well as Gavner. Hatred flared in my chest, and I had to resist the urge to dart back into the action.

Edging clear of the fighting, I would have slipped away, except a crowd of vampires was blocking my path. They'd surrounded a wounded vampaneze and were taunting him before they closed in for the kill. Disgusted by their antics, I looked for another way out. As I was doing that, Arra Sails stepped forward to meet the challenge of the vampaneze called Glalda. Two vampires lay dead at his feet, but Arra pushed on regardless.

"Prepare to die, worm!" she yelled, flicking at him with her chain.

Glalda brushed aside the length of chain and laughed. "So the vampires send women to do their fighting now!" he sneered.

"Women are all the vampaneze are fit to face," Arra retorted. "You are not worthy of facing men and dying with honour. Imagine the disgrace when word spreads that you perished at the hands of a woman!"

"That *would* be a disgrace," Glalda agreed, lunging with his sword. "But it won't happen!"

The two ceased trading words and started trading blows. I was surprised they'd exchanged as much banter as they had — most of the combatants were too concerned with the business of trying to stay alive to stand about like movie stars and swap verbal insults. Arra and the vampaneze circled each other warily, lashing out with their weapons, probing for weak points. Glalda might have been surprised to come face to face with a woman, but he treated her with wary respect. Arra, for her part, was more reckless. She'd mown down several of the panic-stricken vampaneze early in the encounter and had come to believe that all would fall as easily as her initial victims had. She left clumsy defensive gaps and took perilous, needless risks.

I wanted to escape the confines of the cave and put the fighting behind me, but I couldn't bring myself to leave until I'd seen Arra's encounter through to the end. She'd been a good friend and had come looking for me when I went missing. I didn't want to slip away until I knew she was safe.

Mr Crepsley also stopped to observe Arra's battle. He was quite a distance away, separated from her by a pack of scuffling vampires and vampaneze. "Arra!" he yelled. "Do you need help?"

"Not I!" she laughed, driving her chain at the face of the vampaneze. "I'll finish this fool off before you can say—"

Whatever boast she was about to make was cut short. Ducking out of the way of her chain, Glalda brushed her defensive stroke aside, drove the tip of his sword deep into her belly, and twisted cruelly. Arra cried out with anguish and fell.

"Now, *woman*," the vampaneze sneered, straddling her and raising his sword. "Watch closely — I'll show you how we dispose of your kind!" Aiming the tip of his sword at her eyes, he brought it down slowly. Arra could do nothing but stare up at him hatefully and wait to die.

CHAPTER SEVENTEEN

I COULDN'T stand by and let Glalda kill Arra. Darting forward, I threw myself against the vampaneze and knocked him off-balance. He swore, fell heavily, and turned to deal with me. But I was quicker with my light dagger than he was with his heavy sword. Diving on top of him, I stuck it into his chest and by luck pierced his heart.

This vampaneze didn't die quietly like the first one I'd killed. He shook and gibbered madly, then rolled over, dragging me with him. He tried clambering to his feet. It was hopeless — it must have been clear to him that he was going to die — but he made the effort anyway.

When his legs gave out, he collapsed on top of me, almost spearing me with the handle of my own dagger. I gasped for breath beneath him as he convulsed and moaned, then managed to heave him off and slide out. As I got to my knees, I saw his face relax and the life leave his body. I paused and studied him. His expression was much like Gavner's had been — surprised ... annoyed ... afraid.

Gently, I closed the dead warrior's eyelids, then made the death's touch sign by pressing my middle fingers to my forehead and eyes, and spreading my thumb and little finger wide. "Even in death, may you be triumphant," I whispered.

Then I went to check on Arra. She was in a bad way. She tried getting up but I held her down and made her press her hands over the wound in her belly to stop the flow of blood.

"Will I ... die?" Arra gasped, her lips thin with pain.

"Of course not," I said, only for her to grab my hands and glare at me.

"*Will I die?*" she barked.

"I don't know," I answered honestly this time. "Maybe."

She sighed and lay back. "At least I will not die unavenged. You fight well, Darren Shan. You are a true vampire."

"Thanks," I said hollowly.

Mr Crepsley reached us and examined Arra worriedly. He rubbed spit around the edges of the cut, to stop the bleeding, but his efforts didn't make much of a difference. "Does it hurt?" he asked.

"Talk about asking ... stupid questions!" she gurgled.

"You always said I had a knack for putting my foot in my mouth," he smiled, tenderly wiping blood away from the corners of her lips.

"I'd ask you to kiss me," she said, "only I'm not ... in any shape ... for it."

"There'll be plenty of time for kissing later," he vowed.

"Maybe," Arra sighed. "Maybe."

While Mr Crepsley tended to Arra, I sat back and watched numbly as the battle drew to its bloody conclusion. No more than six or seven vampaneze were left on their feet, and each was encircled by several vampires. They should have surrendered, but I knew they wouldn't. Vampires and vampaneze only knew how to win and how to die. For the proud legions of the undead, there was no in-between.

As I watched, two vampaneze who'd been fighting back to back made a break for the exit tunnel. A pack of vampires moved to intercept them, Vanez Blane among them. They prevented the break-out, but one of the vampaneze threw his dagger in spiteful desperation before the vampires captured and killed him. It scorched through the air like a guided missile at its helpless target — *Vanez!*

The games master whipped his head backwards and almost avoided the dagger, but it was too swift, and the tip of the blade snagged on his one good eye. Blood spurted, Vanez screamed and covered his face with his hands, and Seba Nile hurried forward to lead him away to safety.

By the way he'd screamed, I knew in my gut that if Vanez survived, he would never again see the light of the moon or the twinkle of the stars. The vampaneze had finished the job which a lion had started. Vanez was now completely blind.

Glancing around miserably, I saw Streak chewing on the head of a still living vampaneze. One of the younger wolves was helping him. I searched for the other hot-blooded wolf and found it lying dead by a wall, belly ripped open, fangs bared in a vicious death-snarl.

Paris Skyle arrived and took Mika's place. The ancient Prince wielded a thick staff, both ends of which had been sharpened to stake-like points. He showed less taste for the fight than his younger brethren, but still fell in with the bloodshed and latched on to one of the last vampaneze. He made no calls for peace, nor did he tell his men to take these final hardy fighters alive. Perhaps it was best that he didn't. Those vampaneze who'd been taken intact — there were several — had only the Hall of Death to look forward to, where they'd be impaled on stakes in front of a crowd of jeering vampires. Given the choice, I was sure they'd rather die on their feet, with honour.

Finally, painfully, the fighting drew to a close. The last vampaneze was dispatched — he roared as he died, "May the demons take you all!" — and the clearing away of the bodies began. The vampires acted with mechanical efficiency. Generals who'd been swinging axes and swords mere moments before, now picked up wounded vampires and led them away to be nursed, chuckling as they did so, discussing the battle and making light of the injured party's wounds. Others collected the dead, first the fallen vampires, then the vampaneze. They made mounds of the bodies, which were collected by the ghoulish Guardians of the Blood (they must have been waiting outside the cave during the battle), who carried them away to be readied for cremation.

It was all done in good spirits. It didn't bother the Generals that we'd lost nine or ten of our own (the actual death toll, by the time those with fatal injuries succumbed, was twelve). The battle had been won, the vampaneze had been destroyed, and the mountain was secure. They thought they'd come out of 'the scrap' rather well.

A stretcher had to be brought for Arra — there was no way she could walk. She'd grown quieter while waiting, and stared at the roof of the cave as though studying a painting. "Darren," she whispered.

"Yes?"

"Do you remember ... when I beat you ... on the bars?"

"Of course," I smiled.

"You put up ... a good fight."

"Not good enough," I chuckled weakly.

Coughing, she faced Mr Crepsley. "Don't let them kill him, Larten!" she hissed. "I was one of those ... who insisted on his ... death when he failed ... the Trials. But tell them I said he should ... be spared. He's a ... worthy vampire. He's earned a ... reprieve. *Tell* them!"

"You can tell them yourself," Mr Crepsley said, tears dripping down his cheeks, a display of emotion I never thought I'd see. "You will recover. I will take you to the Hall of Princes. *You* can speak up for him."

"Maybe," Arra sighed. "But if I don't ... you'll do it for me? You'll tell them ... what I said? You'll protect him?"

Mr Crepsley nodded wordlessly.

The stretcher arrived and Arra was loaded on to it by two

vampires. Mr Crepsley walked along beside her, holding her hand, trying to comfort her. She made a death's touch sign at me with her free hand as she left, then laughed — blood sprayed from her lips — and winked.

Later that day, shortly before the sun sank in the wintry sky, despite the best efforts of the medics, Arra Sails closed her eyes, made her peace with the gods of the vampires, breathed her last ... and died.

CHAPTER EIGHTEEN

HOURS LATER, when word reached me of Arra's death, I returned to the cave to try and make sense of it all inside my head. The vampires had departed. The dead bodies had been cleared away by the morbid Guardians of the Blood. Even the many trampled spiders had been removed. Only the blood remained, great ugly pools of it, seeping through the cracks in the floor, drying on the walls, dripping from the roof.

I scratched my cheeks — caked in dust, dried blood and tears — and studied the random patterns of blood on the floor and walls as it congealed, thinking back over the fighting and the lives I'd taken. As I listened to the echoes of the dripping blood, I found myself reliving the screams of the vampaneze and vampires, the moans of the dying, Seba leading the blind Vanez away, the relish with which the battle had been fought, Glalda's expression when I killed him, Arra and the way she'd winked at me.

"Mind if I join you?" someone asked.

Glancing up, I saw it was the aged quartermaster of Vampire Mountain, Seba Nile, limping badly from a wound he'd sustained during the fighting. "Be my guest," I said hollowly, and he sat down beside me.

For a few minutes we stared around the crimson-splashed cave in silence. Finally, I asked Seba if he'd heard about Arra's death.

"Yes," he said softly. He laid a hand on my knee. "You must not mourn too grievously for her, Darren. She died proudly, as she would have wished."

"She died stupidly!" I snapped.

"You should not say that," Seba admonished me gently.

"Why not?" I shouted. "It's the truth! This was a stupid fight, fought by stupid people."

"Arra did not think so," Seba said. "She gave her life for this 'stupid fight'. Others gave theirs too."

"That's what makes it stupid," I groaned. "We could have driven them off. We didn't have to come down here and cut them to pieces."

"If I remember correctly," Seba said, "it was *your* novel idea regarding the spiders which paved the way for our attack."

"Thanks for reminding me," I said bitterly, and lapsed back into silence.

"You must not take it to heart," Seba said. "Fighting is our way. It is how we judge ourselves. To the uninitiated this might look like a barbaric bloodbath, but our cause was just.

The vampaneze were plotting our downfall. It was us or them. You know that better than anybody — you were there when they killed Gavner Purl."

"I know," I sighed. "I'm not saying they didn't deserve it. But *why* were they here? *Why* did they invade?"

Seba shrugged. "Doubtless we will unearth the truth once we have had a chance to interrogate the survivors."

"You mean *torture*," I snorted.

"If that is what you want to call it," he replied bleakly.

"OK," I said. "We'll torture them and maybe learn that they attacked just for the hell of it, to knock us out of shape and take over the mountain. Everything will be fine then. We can walk around proudly and slap ourselves on the back.

"But what if that *wasn't* why they attacked?" I pressed. "What if there was a different reason?"

"Such as?" Seba asked.

"I don't know. I've no idea how the vampaneze think or why they do what they do. The point is, neither do *you* or the other vampires. This attack came as a surprise to everyone, didn't it?"

"It was unexpected," Seba agreed. "The vampaneze have never attacked us this aggressively before. Even when they split from us, they cared only about establishing their own society, not undermining ours."

"So why did they do it?" I asked again. "Do you know?"

"No," Seba said.

"There!" I exclaimed. "You don't know, I don't know, the Princes don't know." I got to my knees and locked eyes with him.

"Don't you think somebody should have *asked*? We stormed down here and tore them apart, and not once did any of us stop to question their motives. We reacted like wild animals."

"There was no time for questions," Seba insisted, but I could tell he was troubled by my words.

"Maybe there wasn't," I said. "Not *now*. But what about six months ago? A year? Ten years? A hundred? Kurda was the only one who contacted the vampaneze and tried to understand them. Why didn't others help him? Why weren't attempts made to befriend them, to prevent something like this from ever happening?"

"You are commending Kurda Smahlt?" Seba asked distastefully.

"No. Kurda betrayed us. There's no defending what he did. What I'm saying is — if *we'd* made the effort to get to know the vampaneze, perhaps there would have been no need for *him* to betray us. Maybe we somehow forced his hand."

"Your way of thinking puzzles me," Seba said. "You are more human than vampire, I suppose. In time you will learn to see things our way and—"

"No!" I shouted, jumping up. "I don't want to see things your way. *Your* way is the *wrong* way. I admire the strength, honesty and loyalty of the vampires, and want to fit in as one. But not if it means abandoning myself to stupidity, not if it means turning a blind eye to wisdom and common sense, not if it means enduring bloody messes like this just because my leaders are too proud to sit down with the vampaneze and thrash out their differences."

"It might have been impossible to 'thrash out their differences'," Seba noted.

"But the effort should have been made. The Princes should have *tried*."

Seba shook his head wearily. "Perhaps you are right. I am old and stuck in the past. I remember when vampires had no choices, when it was kill or be killed, fight or perish. From where I stand, today's battle was savage, but no worse than a hundred others I have witnessed over the course of my centuries.

"Having said that, I must admit that the world has changed. Perhaps it is time for us to change too." He smiled. "But who will lead us out of the darkness of the past? Kurda was the face of our future. He, perhaps, could have altered our ways of thinking and living. Now that he has shamed himself, who will dare speak up for the new world and its ways?"

"I don't know," I said. "But somebody should. If they don't, nothing will change, and today's debacle will be repeated, over and over, until the vampires wipe the vampaneze out, or vice versa."

"Heavy thoughts," Seba sighed, then stood and massaged his injured left thigh. "However, I did not come to discuss the future. We have a more immediate and less troubling decision to make."

"What do you mean?" I asked.

He pointed to the floor and I realized that Madam Octa and the spider with light grey spots on his back were squatting behind us. "Many of our eight-legged friends were crushed in the fighting," Seba said. "These were among the survivors. They could have slipped away with the rest, but remained, as though awaiting further orders."

"Do you think that guy's sweet on her?" I asked, pointing to the grey-spotted spider, momentarily forgetting my darker concerns.

"Most certainly," Seba grinned. "I do not think spiders know love as we do. But he remained by her side throughout the fighting, and did not leave when she decided to stay. I think they wish to couple."

I smiled at the absurd notion of Madam Octa walking down an aisle in a tiny white dress, Mr Crepsley waiting at the end to give her away. "You think I should put him in her cage?" I asked.

"Actually, I was thinking along the lines of freeing her, so that she could make her home with him. I am opposed to the captivity of wild creatures, except where strictly necessary."

"You want me to let her go?" I chewed my lower lip and thought it over. "What if she bites someone?"

"I do not think she will," he said. "With all the mountain tunnels to pick from, it is unlikely that she will choose to set up home where people might intrude."

"What about offspring? If she breeds, she could give rise to an army of poisonous spiders."

"I doubt it," Seba smiled. "Even if she could breed with Ba'Halen's spiders, her offspring would probably be no more poisonous than their fathers."

I considered it a while longer. Seba had suggested letting Madam Octa go before, and I had disagreed. But after all she'd been through, it seemed fitting to release her now. "OK," I said. "You've convinced me."

"You do not want to check with Larten?" Seba asked.

"I think he's got bigger things to worry about," I said, referring to Arra.

"Very well," Seba agreed. "Do you want to tell her the good news, or shall I?"

"I'll do it," I said. "Wait a minute — I'll fetch my flute."

Finding the flute where I'd dropped it, I hurried back, pressed it between my lips, blew soundlessly and sent the thought to Madam Octa: "Go. You're free. Leave."

The spider hesitated, then crawled away, the grey-spotted mountain spider in close attendance. Seba and me watched them until they slipped from sight through a crack in the wall. I'd never have fallen in with Mr Crepsley if not for Madam Octa. She'd played a key part in deciding my ultimate destiny. Though I'd never liked the spider since she bit my best friend, Steve Leopard, now that she'd slid out of my life forever, I felt strangely lonely, as though I'd lost a dear companion.

Shrugging off my peculiar mood, I laid my flute down – I wouldn't be needing it any longer – and told Seba I'd like to return to the Halls. Side by side, silent as a pair of ghosts, we turned our backs on the scene of the battle and departed, leaving the pools of blood to settle and thicken as they may.

CHAPTER NINETEEN

UPON REACHING my cell I fell into my hammock, fully clothed, still stained with the blood of the cave. After sleeping rough for so long, it felt heavenly, and I drifted off to sleep almost immediately. I slept right through the night and it was early morning when I awoke. The tunnels were quiet outside. Harkat was awake and waiting for me to get up.

"I heard … you killed … two vampaneze," he said, handing me a bucket of cold water, a rough towel, and a batch of fresh clothes. I grunted in reply, undressed and washed off the dried, flaky blood.

"The vampires … would not let me … join in. I was glad … in a way. I do not … enjoy the thought … of killing."

"There's little about it to enjoy," I agreed.

"Was it … awful?" he asked.

"I don't want to talk about it," I said.

"Very well. I will not … ask again."

I smiled gratefully, dunked my bald head in the bucket, shook off the water when I came up, scrubbed behind my ears, then asked about Mr Crepsley. The green light in Harkat's round eyes dimmed slightly. "He is still … with Arra. He is refusing … to leave her side. Seba is with … him, trying to … comfort him."

"Do you think I should go and have a word?"

Harkat shook his head. "Not at the … moment. Later, he will … need you. For now, let him … grieve alone."

Drying myself off, I asked about Vanez and the other vampires, but Harkat wasn't able to tell me much. He knew at least ten vampires had died and more were seriously injured, but word of who they were hadn't reached him.

Once dressed, I accompanied Harkat to the Hall of Khledon Lurt for a quick meal, then we wandered back to our cell and stayed there for the rest of the day. We could have mixed with the vampires in the Hall – they'd cheered loudly when they saw me coming in – but I didn't want to sit listening to them spinning wild tales about the battle and how we'd obliterated the vampaneze.

Finally, towards dusk, Mr Crepsley staggered into our cell. His face was paler than usual as he slumped into my hammock, lowered his head into his hands and groaned. "You heard the news?" he whispered.

"Yes," I said. Then, after a brief pause, I added weakly, "Sorry."

"I thought she was going to make it," he sighed. "I knew the wound was fatal, but she lasted such a long time, defying the odds, I began to believe she would live."

"Has she…" I cleared my throat. "Has she been cremated yet?"

He shook his head. "Nobody has. The Guardians of the Blood are holding the bodies aside for at least two days and nights, as is our custom. The vampaneze, on the other hand…" He lowered his hands and his expression was genuinely frightening. "*They* are being fed to the flames at this very moment. We took them from the Guardians and cut them up into tiny pieces, so their souls cannot escape the pull of the Earth — they will never make it to Paradise. I hope they rot here for all eternity."

I sensed this wasn't the right time to speak of the disgust I'd felt in the cave, or my belief that vampires needed to learn compassion, so I held my tongue and nodded quickly.

"What about … Kurda and the … other survivors?" Harkat asked.

"They will be dealt with later," Mr Crepsley said, eyes narrowing. "They will be questioned first, then executed. I will be there when they are. Do either of you wish to attend?"

"The questioning, yes," I said. "I'm not so sure about the executions."

"I will give … both a miss," Harkat said. "I don't feel … it's my place … to watch. This is a … matter for vampires."

"As you wish," Mr Crepsley said. "What about the funerals? Do you want to bid farewell to Arra?"

"Of course," I answered quietly.

"I would like … that," Harkat agreed.

Mr Crepsley's expression had softened as he mentioned Arra's name. "She did not say much once she left the cave," he whispered, more to himself than to Harkat or me. "Speaking was painful. She conserved her energy. Fought hard. She clung on to life as long as she could.

"The medics expected her to die. Every time her breath caught in her throat, they rushed forward, eager to clear the way for other wounded vampires. But she hung on. They got so accustomed to the false alarms that when she did eventually die, they did not realize, and she lay there twenty minutes, serene in my embrace, smiling blankly at me."

His eyes had filled with tears. I handed him a scrap of cloth as they began to drip, but he didn't use it. "I couldn't hear her last words," he croaked. "She spoke too softly. I think she was making some kind of reference to the bars."

"Have you had any sleep?" I asked, beginning to cry myself.

"How can I sleep?" he sighed. "There are the inquisitions to prepare for. I will not miss Kurda's sentencing, not if I have to forsake sleep forever."

"Don't be silly," I gently chided him. "When does the questioning start?"

"Midnight," he sniffed.

"Then you've plenty of time. Grab some sleep. I'll wake you before it starts and we'll go together."

"Promise?" he asked.

"I wouldn't lie to you about something this important," I replied.

He nodded, rose, and started for his cell. In the doorway, he paused and looked back. "You did well in the cave, Darren. You fought bravely. I was proud of you."

"Thanks," I said, choking on my tears, which were flowing freely now.

"Proud," he muttered again, then faced the corridor and shuffled off to his cell, carrying himself like an old, tired, broken man.

Later that night, Kurda Smahlt's trial began.

The Hall of Princes was packed with furious, bitter vampires, as was the cave outside. Virtually every vampire in the mountain wanted to be there to jeer at the traitor, spit at him, and cheer his sentence when it was announced. I'd come with Mr Crepsley and Seba Nile. We were seated in the front row. We hadn't thought we'd get so close — we arrived late — but I soon discovered that I was the flavour of the moment. The vampires attributed much of their victory over the vampaneze to my endeavours. They roared with rough delight when they saw me, and ushered me forward, pushing Mr Crepsley and Seba along with me, insisting I take pride of place. I'd have rather hung back and viewed the proceedings from afar, but Mr Crepsley was anxious to get as close to the platform as possible, and I hadn't the heart to disappoint him, not after what he'd been through with Arra.

The conspirators were to be brought forward one by one, for separate questioning and sentencing. If they spoke openly, and the Princes were satisfied with their answers, they'd be taken straight to the Hall of Death and executed. If they refused to co-operate, they'd be led away and tortured in the hope that they'd spill their secrets (but vampaneze, like vampires, could deal with enormous amounts of pain, and were almost impossible to break).

The first to face trial was Kurda. The disgraced General was dragged forward in chains, past the ranks of hissing and screaming vampires. Some brushed his guards aside and struck or kicked him. A few pulled at his blond hair and yanked fistfuls of it out by the roots. By the time he reached the platform, he was in a sorry state, his white robes ripped, his body bruised and bleeding. Yet still he held his head high, reacting to none of the abuse.

The Princes were waiting for him on the platform, flanked by four guards with long, sharp spears. He was placed before the trio, each of whom spat contemptuously on him. Then he was led to one side and turned around to face the assembled vampires. At first I couldn't bring myself to look him in the eye, but when I finally worked up the courage, I found he was staring down at me, smiling sadly.

"Order!" Mika Ver Leth shouted, silencing the booing vampires. "We have a long night ahead of us. We want to settle each case as quickly and effortlessly as possible. I know feelings are running high, but anyone who interrupts our interrogation of Kurda Smahlt – or the others – will be ejected immediately. Have I made myself clear?"

The vampires muttered sullenly and settled back in their seats. When peace had been restored, Paris Skyle rose and addressed the congregation. "We know why we are here," he spoke softly. "We have been betrayed and besieged. I am as eager as any to see the vile curs suffer for their crimes, but first we must learn why they attacked and if we can expect further assaults." Turning to Kurda, his features hardened. "Were you in league with the vampaneze we killed yesterday?" he asked.

There was a long pause. Then Kurda nodded and said, "I was."

Several vampires screamed bloody murder, and were swiftly escorted out of the Hall. The others sat white-faced and trembling, glaring hatefully at Kurda.

"Upon whose orders were you acting?" Paris asked.

"My own," Kurda said.

"Liar!" Arrow barked. "Tell us who set you up to this, or so help me, I'll—"

"I know what you'll do," Kurda interrupted. "Don't worry — I have no wish to be subjected to the rougher questioning of your professional torturers. I will speak the truth here."

"You'd better," Arrow grumbled, sinking back on his throne.

"Upon whose orders were you acting?" Paris asked again.

"My own," Kurda repeated. "The plan was mine. The vampaneze were here at my bidding. Torture me all you wish — my answer won't change because it can't change. It's the truth."

"*You* dreamt up this outrage?" Mika asked incredulously.

"I did," Kurda nodded. "I arranged for the vampaneze to

come. I provided them with copies of my maps, so they could slip in undetected. I—"

"Traitor!" a vampire howled, and tried to rush the platform. He was intercepted by a couple of guards and hauled away, kicking and screaming for all his worth.

"I could reach him," Mr Crepsley hissed in the midst of the commotion, his eyes pinned on Kurda. "I could leap forward now and make an end of him before anyone could stop me."

"Peace, Larten," Seba whispered, laying a soothing hand on the vampire's trembling shoulders. "Kurda is going nowhere. His death will come soon enough. Let us hear him out."

As soon as the screams of the irate protestor had subsided, Paris resumed the questioning. "Is it true that you planned to slip the vampaneze into the Hall of Princes once you had been invested, to seize control of the Stone of Blood?"

"It is," Kurda answered directly. "We would have waited for the Ceremony of Conclusion. Then, while you were drinking yourselves stupid, reminiscing about this Council and looking forward to the next, I'd have sneaked them up through secret tunnels, made short work of those who stood on guard, and taken over the Hall."

"But you could not have held it," Paris objected. "Surely you knew that Mika, Arrow and I would force open the doors and overwhelm you."

"That would not have happened," Kurda disagreed. "You wouldn't have been alive to force open the doors. I was going to poison the three of you. I'd six bottles of a very rare wine set aside especially for the occasion, each spiked with a particularly lethal concoction. I would have presented them to the three of you in advance of the Ceremony. You'd have toasted my good health, died an hour or two later, and the Hall would have been mine."

"And then you would have set about getting rid of the rest of our kind," Arrow growled.

"No," Kurda said. "I would have set about *saving* them."

"What do you mean?" Paris asked, surprised.

"Has nobody wondered why I chose such an inopportune moment to instigate an attack?" Kurda asked, addressing the question to the entire Hall. "Doesn't it seem strange that I opted to sneak in a horde of vampaneze during Council, while these Halls and tunnels were packed with vampires, when the chance of their being discovered was far greater than if they'd come in a few months' time?"

Paris looked confused. "I assumed you wanted to strike while we were all gathered together," he muttered.

"Why?" Kurda challenged him. "The plan was to sneak into the Hall and seize the Stone of Blood, not to engage the vampire forces. The more vampires in the mountain, the more difficult our task."

"You wanted to rub it in," Arrow snorted. "You wanted to show off and be able to say you took the Halls in the middle of Council."

"You think I'm that vain?" Kurda laughed. "You think I'd have risked my life just to look stylish? You forget — I'm not like most vampires. I act for the sake of results, not appearances. I'm a cold conspirator, not a hot-headed braggart. I was only interested in success, not showmanship."

"So why *did* you attack now?" Mika asked, exasperated.

"Because we'd run out of time," Kurda sighed. "It was now or never. As I said, I meant to save our race, not vanquish it. Our only hope lay in an immediate, pre-emptive strike. Now that it has failed, I fear we are doomed."

"What's this nonsense about pre-emptive strikes?" Arrow snapped. "We had no intention of attacking the vampaneze."

"It was not an attack by the vampires on the vampaneze I sought to halt," Kurda explained. "It was an attack by the vampaneze on the vampires."

"He talks in riddles!" Arrow exploded angrily. "He attacked *with* the vampaneze to prevent an attack *by* the vampaneze? Rubbish!"

"Perhaps he's mad," Mika murmured seriously.

"If only," Kurda chuckled darkly.

"This is getting us nowhere," Arrow growled. "I say we take him below and drain the truth out of him, drop by bloody drop. He's playing us for fools. We should—"

"Mr Tiny has visited the vampaneze," Kurda said, and though he didn't raise his voice, it was as though he'd roared. Arrow and the rest of the vampires lapsed into a sudden, nervous silence, and waited for him to continue. "He came three years ago," Kurda said in that same quiet but foreboding tone. "He told them that the Vampaneze Lord walked the lands and that they should search for him. When word reached me, I dedicated myself to the task of reuniting the vampires with the vampaneze. I hoped that if we bonded before they discovered their mythical leader, we could avoid the terrible consequences of Mr Tiny's prophecy."

"I thought you did not believe the myth of the Vampaneze Lord," Paris noted.

"I didn't," Kurda agreed, "until I saw how seriously the vampaneze were taking it. They'd never been interested in war with us, but since Mr Tiny's visit, they've been strengthening their arsenals and recruiting vigorously, preparing for their fabled leader's coming.

"And now he *has* come." A physical shock ran through the Hall. The vampires recoiled in their seats as though struck, and their faces became ashen. "Six months ago, the Vampaneze Lord was discovered," Kurda said, dropping his gaze. "He hasn't been blooded, but he's taken his place among them and is learning their ways. My act of treachery was the last desperate roll of the dice. If I'd gained control of the Stone of Blood, I might have been able to win the vampaneze over — not all of our blood-cousins are eager to engage in a war with us. Now that I've failed, the way is open for him. He'll be blooded, take control of the vampaneze, and lead them against us. And he'll win."

Lowering his voice, Kurda muttered ironically, "Congratulations, gentlemen. After today's *great victory*, nothing stands between your good selves and a futile war with the vampaneze. You've cleared the way for Mr Tiny's prophecy to come to pass.

"Enjoy your celebrations. This may be the last chance you get to bang your drums and brag about your valour. As of tonight, the clock is ticking. When it stops, our time is finished. Every vampire in this Hall — on this world — is *damned*."

Smiling bitterly, Kurda snapped loose the chains around his right hand, brought his fingers to his forehead and eyes, and made the death's touch sign at the Princes. Then he looked at me and repeated the gesture. "Even in death, may you be triumphant," he croaked sarcastically, and angry, desolate tears glittered in the corners of his sad blue eyes.

CHAPTER TWENTY

THE AWFUL hush which followed Kurda's proclamation seemed to last an eternity. Finally, Seba Nile rose slowly, pointed a trembling finger at Kurda, and hissed, "You lie!"

Kurda shook his head stubbornly. "I don't."

"You have *seen* this Vampaneze Lord?" Seba asked.

"No," Kurda said. "I would have killed him if I had."

"Then how do you know he exists?"

Kurda shrugged in response.

"Answer him!" Paris thundered.

"The vampaneze have a unique coffin," Kurda said. "They call it the Coffin of Fire. Mr Tiny bestowed it upon them many centuries ago, around the same time that he gave us this magical dome in which we stand. It has been guarded by a troop of vampaneze ever since, who call themselves the Carriers of Destiny.

"The coffin is like any other — until someone lies down

in it and the lid is put in place. Then the coffin fills with a terrible fire. If the person is destined to lead the vampaneze, he will emerge unscathed. Otherwise, he perishes in the flames.

"Over the decades, many vampaneze have braved the Coffin of Fire — and died. But six months ago a human lay down in it, faced the flames, and came out whole. He is the Lord of the Vampaneze, and once he has been blooded, every member of the clan will obey and follow him — to the death, if required."

The Princes stared at Kurda uncertainly, fearfully, until Paris asked in a whisper, "Were you there when this human was tested?"

"No," Kurda replied. "Only the Carriers of Destiny were present."

"Then this might be only a rumour," Paris said hopefully. "A fanciful lie."

"Vampaneze never lie," Kurda reminded him.

"Perhaps they've changed," Mika mused. "The Stone of Blood would be worth a few lies. They could have tricked you, Kurda."

Again Kurda shook his head. "Many vampaneze are as troubled by the coming of their Lord as we are. They don't seek a war. They fear the losses such a struggle would incur. That's why thirty-eight agreed to accompany me on this mission. They hoped to prevent total, all-out conflict, sparing their colleagues and friends."

"You keep talking about *preventing* a war and *saving* us,"

Paris noted. "I do not see how you thought betraying our cause could be of any help."

"I intended to force a union," Kurda explained. "When I heard that the Vampaneze Lord had been unearthed, I knew it was too late to put in place a fair peace agreement. Weighing up my options — which were few — I decided to chance a coup. Had I succeeded, vampires everywhere would have been at the mercy of the vampaneze. Those in the Hall of Princes could have communicated with their kin and, via the Stone of Blood, fed them the exact location of most living vampires. Our people would have had no choice but to agree to my terms."

"And what would *they* have been?" Paris asked contemptuously.

"That we join the ranks of the vampaneze," Kurda answered. "I'd hoped for an equal union, where vampires and vampaneze each made concessions. Given the change of circumstances, that was impossible. We'd have had to adopt the vampaneze ways and customs. But that would have been preferable to annihilation."

"Not for me," Arrow growled. "I'd have rather died."

"I'm sure others would too," Kurda agreed. "But I believe most would have seen sense. Even if they hadn't, and you all chose to fight to the death, at least I'd have tried."

"What was in it for *you*, Kurda?" Mika asked. "Did the vampaneze promise you a title? Are there to be Princes in the new regime?"

"The vampaneze made no offers," Kurda replied shortly. "Many wish to avoid a war, so a few dozen volunteers — brave men, who you killed like vermin — agreed to risk their lives and assist me. We had no ulterior motives. We did it for your sakes, not our own."

"Very noble of you, Kurda," Mika sneered.

"Nobler than you imagine!" Kurda snapped, losing his cool. "Have you no brains? Don't you see the sacrifice I made?"

"What sacrifice?" Mika asked, taken aback.

"Win or lose," Kurda said, "my reward would have been death. The vampaneze despise traitors even more than we do. Had everything worked out, I'd have remained within the Hall of Princes to oversee the merging of the clans. Then, when our people's future was assured, I'd have offered myself for sentencing and suffered the very same fate which awaits me now."

"You expect us to believe the vampaneze would have killed the man who presented their arch-enemies to them?" Mika laughed.

"You'll believe it because it's true," Kurda said. "Neither the vampires nor vampaneze will suffer a traitor to live. That law is written in the hearts of each and every member of the clans. The vampaneze who came with me would have been heroes — they'd broken none of their own laws, except trespassing on vampire turf — but *me*, a man who'd betrayed his own?" Kurda shook his head. "There was nothing 'in it' for me, Mika, and more fool you if you believe any different."

Kurda's words disturbed the vampires. I saw them gazing around at one another, ominous questions in their eyes and on their tongues. "Perhaps he wants us to reward him instead of dropping him on the stakes," someone cackled, but no one laughed.

"I expect and ask for no mercy," Kurda responded. "My only wish is that you remember what I tried to do in the difficult years to come. I had only the best interests of the clan at heart. I hope one night you see that and acknowledge it."

"If all you have said is true," Paris Skyle commented, "why did you not come to *us*? If we had known about the Vampaneze Lord, we could have taken steps to stamp him out."

"By killing every living vampaneze?" Kurda asked bitterly.

"If we had to," Paris nodded.

"That was not my wish," Kurda sighed. "I sought to save lives, not take them. Fighting won't save the vampires, not if Mr Tiny's prophecy is valid. But a *union* – before the threat could come to pass – might have been the saving of us.

"I can't say I was right," Kurda continued. "For all I know, my actions will provide the spark which leads to war and destruction. But I had to try. I believed it was in my hands to divert the course of fate. Right or wrong, I couldn't willingly surrender my people to Mr Tiny's grim prophecy."

Kurda trained his gaze on me. "I have few regrets," he said. "I took a chance and it didn't pan out — that's life. My one real source of sorrow is that I had to kill Gavner Purl. It was not my wish to shed blood. But the plan came first. The future of our people as a whole outweighed that of any individual. I'd have killed a dozen more like Gavner if I had to — even a hundred, if it meant safeguarding the lives of the rest."

With that, Kurda drew his case to a close and refused to speak any more of his betrayal. The Princes asked him if he knew where the Vampaneze Lord was, or what the vampaneze were planning, but in answer he just shook his head.

The Princes opened the questioning to the floor, but none of the vampires accepted the invitation to address the fallen General. They looked downcast and ashamed of themselves now. None of them liked Kurda or approved of what he'd done, but they had come to respect him, and regretted the way they'd treated him earlier.

When a suitable period of silence had elapsed, Paris nodded at the guards on the platform to position Kurda before the Princes. When he was standing in front of them, Paris reflected inwardly for a few minutes, gathering his thoughts. When ready, he spoke. "I am troubled by what you have said. I would rather you had been a nefarious traitor, out for profit and personal gain. That way I could sentence you to death with a clear conscience and no hesitation.

"I believe you acted in good faith. It may even be as you say, that by thwarting your plans, we have condemned ourselves to defeat at the hands of the vampaneze. Maybe it would have been for the best if Darren had not chanced upon your colleagues in the cave, or survived to carry news of them back.

"But you *were* discovered, you *were* revealed, and the vampaneze *were* dispatched by all bloody means possible. There is no way to change these things, even if we wished to. The future may be bleak, but we shall face it on our feet, as vampires, with firm hearts and wills, as is our way.

"I have sympathy for you, Kurda," he continued. "You acted as you thought you must, without consideration for yourself, and for that you are to be commended. However, you also acted without consideration for our laws and ways, and for that you must be punished. There is only one fitting punishment for the crime you have committed, and it is absolute — *execution*."

A heavy collective sigh swept through the Hall. "Had I a choice," Paris went on, "I would grant you the right to die on your feet, as a vampire, with pride. You do not deserve to die ignominiously, bound and blindfolded, impaled on stakes from behind. I would let you embark on a series of harsh tests, one after the other, until you perished honourably. And I would drink a toast to your name as you were being cremated whole.

"But, as a Prince, I have no choice. Whatever your reasons, you betrayed us, and that harsh fact of life takes precedence over my own wishes." Rising, Paris pointed at Kurda and said, "I vote that he be taken to the Hall of Death and summarily executed. After that, he should be dismembered before cremation, so that his soul may never know Paradise."

After a brief pause, Mika Ver Leth stood and pointed as Paris was pointing. "I don't know if it's just or not," he sighed, "but we must obey the customs which guide and maintain us. I too vote for the Hall of Death and shameful cremation."

Arrow stood and pointed. "The Hall of Death," he said simply.

"Does anyone care to speak on behalf of the traitor?" Paris asked. There was complete silence. "We may be persuaded to reconsider our judgement if there is opposition," he said. Still no one spoke.

I stared at the pitiful figure in front of me and thought of how he'd made me feel at home when I arrived at Vampire Mountain, how he'd treated me like a friend, joked with me and shared his knowledge and years of experience. I remembered when he knocked Arra Sails off the bars, and how he'd offered his hand to her, the look of hurt on his face when she refused to take it. I recalled how he'd saved my life and gone out on a limb for my sake, risking even the success of his mission to help me out of a jam. I wouldn't be here now, alive, if not for Kurda Smahlt.

I started to rise, to speak up for him and request a less horrible form of retribution. Then Gavner's face flashed through my mind, and Arra's, and I stopped to think what he'd have done if Mr Crepsley, Seba or any others had got in his way. He would have killed all of them if he'd had to. He wouldn't have taken pleasure in it, but he wouldn't have baulked either. He'd have done what he felt needed to be done, the same as any true-hearted vampire.

Sinking back, I shook my head miserably and held my tongue. This was too big. It wasn't for me to decide. Kurda had fashioned his own downfall. He must stand alone to face it. I felt lousy, not sticking up for him, but I'd have felt just as lousy if I had.

When it became apparent that the judgement of the Princes was not going to be called into question, Paris signalled the guards on the platform, who surrounded Kurda and stripped him bare. Kurda said nothing as they robbed him of his clothes and pride, just gazed up at the roof of the Hall.

When Kurda was naked, Paris held his fingers together tight, dipped them in a bowl of snake's blood which had been hidden behind his throne, and ran his hand over Kurda's chest. Mika and Arrow followed suit, leaving three ugly red marks — the sign among the vampires for a traitor or one of bad standing.

Once Kurda had been marked, his guards led him away. Nobody spoke or made a sound. He kept his head bowed low as he exited, but I saw tears dripping down his cheeks as he passed. He was lonely and scared. I wanted to comfort him but it was too late for that. Better to let him pass without delay.

This time, as he was guided past the assembled vampires, nobody jeered or tried to harm him. There was a brief pause when he reached the open doors, to clear the way through the vampires packed beyond, then he was escorted out of the Hall and down through the tunnels to the Hall of Death, where he was caged, blindfolded, raised above the pit of stakes, then brutally and painfully executed. And that was the end of the traitor ... *my friend* ... Kurda Smahlt.

CHAPTER TWENTY-ONE

I DIDN'T go to watch Kurda being killed. Nor did I stick around for the trials of the vampaneze. Instead, I returned to my cell, where I remained until it was time, late the next night, for the funerals of Arra Sails, Gavner Purl and the others who'd died fighting to protect Vampire Mountain. Gavner's body had been recovered after the battle. Kurda told his guards where to find it and a search party soon located it, stuffed into a deep crack far down the mountain.

Streak and his fellow wolves had returned to the pack. They slipped away without a fuss, not long after the fighting had finished, leaving their dead companion behind. I never had a chance to bid them farewell or thank them.

I wondered if I'd ever run with the pack again. It seemed unlikely, even if my life was spared by the Princes. Now that Council was coming to an end, the wolves would be dispersing, to return to their usual hunting grounds. I'd probably seen the last of Streak, Rudi and the rest.

I spent the time between the trials and the funerals working on my diary. I hadn't touched it since coming to Vampire Mountain. I read back over my earlier entries, then described all that had happened to me since I left the Cirque Du Freak and set out for the mountain with Mr Crepsley. I managed to lose myself in the diary, so time flew by. I normally didn't enjoy writing – too much like homework – but once I started telling the story, the words tumbled out with hardly any effort. My pen only paused a couple of times, when I slipped away to eat and caught an hour or two of sleep.

I hoped the writing would help me get things straight in my head, especially with regards to Kurda, but I was just as confused by the end as I'd been at the beginning. No matter how I looked at it, I couldn't help feeling that Kurda had been both a hero *and* a villain. Things would be simpler if he was one or the other, but I couldn't pigeon-hole him. It was just too complicated.

Kurda had wanted to prevent the destruction of the vampires. To that end, he'd betrayed them. Was he evil for doing so? Or would it have been worse to act nobly and let his people perish? Should one stay true to one's friends, whatever the consequences? I found it impossible to decide. Part of me hated Kurda and believed he deserved to be killed; another part remembered his good intentions and amiable manner, and wished there'd been some other way of punishing him, short of execution.

Mr Crepsley came to fetch Harkat and me before I finished writing. I'd got most of the story down, but there was a bit left, so I stuck my pen between a couple of pages to mark my place, laid it aside, and accompanied the sorrowful vampire to the Hall of Cremation to bid farewell to our dear departed friends and allies.

Gavner Purl was the first to be cremated, since he was the first who'd fallen. He'd been dressed in a simple white robe and lay on a thin stretcher in the cremation pit. He looked peaceful lying there, eyes closed, short brown hair carefully combed, lips worked into a smile by the Guardians of the Blood who'd prepared his body. Though I knew the Guardians had removed all of Gavner's blood, along with most of his internal organs and brains, there were no visible signs of their macabre handiwork.

I started to tell Mr Crepsley what Gavner's final words had been, but as I did, I burst into tears. Mr Crepsley wrapped his arms around me and let me sob into his chest, patting me comfortingly. "Do you want to leave?" he asked.

"No," I moaned. "I want to stay. It's just ... hard, you know?"

"I know," Mr Crepsley said, and by the tears in his own eyes, I knew he meant it.

A large crowd had gathered to see Gavner off. Usually, only one's closest friends or colleagues attended a funeral. Vampires were different to humans — they didn't believe in showing up in large numbers to pay their condolences. But Gavner had been popular and had died to save others, so the cave was full. Even Paris Skyle and Arrow were present. Mika would have been there too, except one had to stay behind to guard the Hall of Princes.

There was no such thing as a vampire priest. Though vampires had their own gods and beliefs, they'd no organized religion. Paris, as the oldest vampire in the chamber, led the brief, simple ceremonies. "His name was Gavner Purl," he chanted, and everyone repeated the Prince's words. "He died with honour." Again we followed suit. "May his spirit find Paradise," he finished, and once we'd echoed his sentiments, the twigs and leaves beneath Gavner were lit by two Guardians, who made peculiar signs over his body, then moved back out of the way.

It didn't take the flames long to consume the General. The Guardians knew their business and had arranged things so the fire grew quickly and made short work of Gavner. I'd never been to a cremation before. To my surprise, I found it wasn't as upsetting as I'd thought it would be. There was something strangely comforting in watching the flames engulf Gavner, the smoke rising and slipping through the cracks in the ceiling, almost as if it was Gavner's spirit departing.

I was glad that I'd come, though I was grateful that we were ushered out of the Hall when it was time to extract Gavner's bones from the ashes and grind them to dust in the bowls which surrounded the pit. I don't think I could have stood by and watched the Guardians doing that.

Three more vampires were to be cremated before it was Arra Sails' turn. While Mr Crepsley, Harkat and me waited outside during the ceremonies, Seba Nile and Vanez Blane appeared, the limping quartermaster leading the blind games master. The pair greeted us and stopped to chat. They apologized for missing Gavner's cremation but Vanez had been undergoing treatment and couldn't leave until the dressing on his bad eye had been changed.

"How is the eye?" Mr Crepsley asked.

"Ruined," Vanez said cheerfully, as though it was no big thing. "I'm blind as a bat now."

"I thought, since you were having it treated..."

"The treatment's to stop infection setting in and spreading to my brain," Vanez explained.

"You don't sound too upset," I noted, staring at the large patch over his right eye, thinking how awful it must be to lose one's sight.

Vanez shrugged. "I'd rather have kept it, but it's not the end of the world. I can still hear, smell and feel my way around. It will take a while to get used to, but I learnt to adapt when I lost the first eye. I'm sure I'll be able to cope without the second."

"Will you leave Vampire Mountain?" Mr Crepsley asked diplomatically.

"No," Vanez said. "Any other time, I'd have gone out into the world and stumbled around until I met with a noble end, as is a blind vampire's way. But the coming of the Vampaneze Lord has changed all that. Paris asked me to stay. I can make myself useful, even if it's only helping out in the stores or kitchens. Right now, every vampire's needed. My remaining will allow some younger, fitter vampire to focus his energies elsewhere and carry the fight to the vampaneze."

"I too shall be staying," Seba announced. "My retirement has been put on hold. The world and its adventures will have to wait. The old and infirm must play their part now, selflessly. This is no time for putting one's best interests before those of the clan."

That phrase gave me a jolt. Kurda had expressed similar sentiments earlier during my stay. He thought it was wrong that crippled or old vampires were discarded by their colleagues. It was horribly ironic that his betrayal and death should serve as the spur to win other vampires round to his way of thinking.

"Does that mean the offer of a job no longer stands?" Mr Crepsley asked Seba — he'd been earmarked to take over as quartermaster when Seba retired.

"It does," Seba said, "but I am sure the Princes will find *some* use for you." He smiled briefly. "A sweeper of floors, perhaps?"

"Perhaps." Mr Crepsley also managed a fleeting smile. "Mika has already asked me about staying and perhaps resuming my official General duties, but I told him I did not wish to consider such things at the moment. I will decide later, when I have had time to mull the situation over."

"What about Darren?" Vanez asked. "Have the Princes declared his fate yet?"

"No," Mr Crepsley said. "Mika promised to reopen the debate first thing after the funeral ceremonies. I am sure he will be pardoned."

"I hope so," Vanez said, but he sounded unsure. "You do know that a death penalty has never been revoked? The Princes would have to alter the laws in order to spare Darren's life."

"Then alter them they shall!" Mr Crepsley growled, taking a step forward in anger.

"Peace, Larten," Seba interceded. "Vanez means no harm. This is an unusual case and it will require much thought before a final decision can be made, one way or the other."

"There is no 'one way or the other'," Mr Crepsley insisted. "I promised Arra I would not let Darren be killed. She said he had earned the right to life, and anyone who would argue with her dying wish will have *me* to deal with. We have endured enough death. I will not stand for any more."

"Hopefully, there will be none," Seba sighed. "I believe the Princes will be sympathetic. They may not wish to bend the laws, but in this case I think they will."

"They had better," Mr Crepsley said, and would have said more, except at that moment Arra was brought forward on a stretcher and carried into the Hall of Cremation. Mr Crepsley stiffened and stared after her longingly. I put an arm around him and so did Seba.

"Be brave, Larten," Seba said. "She would not have wanted emotional outbursts."

"I will conduct myself with all due decorum," Mr Crepsley said pompously, then added beneath his breath, "But I miss her. With all my heart and soul, I miss her."

Once Arra's body had been laid in place, the doors were

opened and we entered, Mr Crepsley in front, Seba, Vanez, Harkat and me just behind, to make our farewells. Mr Crepsley was every bit as composed as he'd sworn he would be. He didn't even shed a tear when the funeral litter was set alight. It was only later, when he was alone in his cell, that he wept aloud, and his cries echoed through the corridors and tunnels of Vampire Mountain, far into the cold, lonely dawn.

CHAPTER TWENTY-TWO

THE LONG wait between the cremations and my trial was grisly. Though Mr Crepsley kept saying I would be pardoned for failing my Trials of Initiation, and forgiven for running away, I wasn't so sure. Working on my diary kept my mind off the forthcoming trial, but once I'd brought it up to date and checked to make sure I hadn't left anything out, there was nothing to do but sit back and twiddle my thumbs.

Finally, two guards appeared and told me the Princes were ready to receive me. I asked for a few minutes to compose myself. They stood outside the door of my cell while I faced Harkat. "Here," I said, handing him a bag (which used to belong to a friend of mine — Sam Grest) with my diary and some personal effects. "If they decide to execute me, I want you to have these."

Harkat nodded solemnly, then followed as I exited the cell and let the guards guide me to the Hall of Princes. Mr

Crepsley also fell in behind, having been notified by a third Mountain guard.

We paused outside the doors of the Hall. My belly was rumbling with fear and I was trembling all over. "Be brave," Mr Crepsley whispered. "The Princes will treat you fairly. In the event that they do not, I shall come to your aid."

"Me too," Harkat said. "I won't let ... them do anything ... crazy to you."

"Thanks," I smiled, "but I don't want either of you to get involved. Things are bad enough as they are. No point all three of us winding up in the Hall of Death!"

The doors opened and we entered.

The vampires within looked solemn and their heavy gazes did nothing to ease my discomfort. Nobody spoke as we marched to the platform, where the Princes sat waiting, stern, arms crossed. The air seemed thin and I had to gasp deeply for breath.

Mr Crepsley and Harkat sat at the base of the platform, next to Seba Nile and Vanez Blane. I was led up on to it, where I stood facing the Vampire Princes. After a short period of silence, Paris Skyle spoke. "These are strange times," he sighed. "For centuries, we vampires have stuck by our old ways and traditions and looked on, amused, as humanity changes and evolves, growing ever more fractured. While the humans of this planet have lost their sense of direction and purpose, our belief in ourselves has never wavered — until recently.

"It is a sign of the times that one vampire would raise his

hand against his brothers, regardless of his good intentions. Treachery is nothing new to mankind, but this is our first real taste of it, and it has left a sour taste in our mouths. It would be easy to turn a blind eye to the traitors and dismiss them from our thoughts. But that would be to ignore the root of our problem and leave the way open for further acts of treason. The truth is that the changing world has made its mark upon us at last, and we must change if we are to survive within it.

"Whilst we have no plans to abandon our ways outright, we must face the future and adapt as required. We have been living in a world of absolutes, but this is no longer the case. We must open our eyes, ears and hearts to new ways of thinking and living.

"That is why we have gathered here tonight. In the normal run of things, there would have been no call for a meeting to decide Darren Shan's fate. He failed the Trials of Initiation — the penalty for which is death. He then fled from sentencing, a crime punishable in only one way — death. In the past, he would have been put to the stakes, and none would have intervened on his behalf.

"But times *have* changed and Darren has played an instrumental part in opening our eyes to the *need* for change. He has endured great pain and sacrificed his freedom for the good of the clan. He has fought bravely and proven his worth. Previously, his reward would have been a noble death. Now, however, pleas have been submitted, arguing for his right to live."

Paris cleared his throat and sipped from a glass of blood. The air in the Hall was alive with tension. I couldn't see the faces of the vampires behind me, but I could feel their eyes boring into my back.

"We have argued your case at great length," Paris recommenced. "In the world of humans, I imagine it would have been easy to reach a conclusion and you would have been openly pardoned. But we view justice differently. To clear your name and free you would mean altering the very fabric of our laws.

"Some have claimed that it is time to fine-tune the laws. They put forward a convincing case on your behalf. They said laws were made to be broken, a sentiment I do not agree with, but which I am beginning to understand. Others wanted the laws pertaining to the Trials of Initiation temporarily waived. In that case, you would have been cleared, then the laws would have been reinstated. A few called for permanent, outright changes. They felt the laws were unfair and – keeping in mind the threat posed by the coming of the Vampaneze Lord – senseless, in that they might work to rob us of new recruits and weaken our hand."

Paris hesitated and ran his fingers through his long, grey beard. "After lengthy debate, much of it heated, we decided against altering our laws. There may come a time when we will have to, but–"

"Charna's guts!" Mr Crepsley roared, and the next thing I knew, he'd jumped on to the platform and was standing in front of me, fists raised. Moments later, Harkat had joined him, and the two faced the Princes and glared. "I will not stand for this!" Mr Crepsley shouted. "Darren risked his life for you, and now you would sentence him to death? Never! I will not tolerate such bloody-minded ingratitude. Anyone wishing to lay hands on my assistant will first have to lay hands on *me*, and I swear by all that is sacred, I will fight them to my last savage breath!"

"The same goes ... for me," Harkat growled, tearing loose the mask from around his mouth, his scarred grey face even more fearsome-looking than usual.

"I expected more self-control, Larten," Paris tutted, not in the least put out. "This is most unlike you."

"Desperate times call for desperate measures," Mr Crepsley retorted. "There is a time for tradition, and there is a time to exercise common sense. I will not let you—"

"Larten," Seba called from the crowd. Mr Crepsley half-turned at the sound of his mentor's voice. "You should hear Paris out," Seba suggested.

"You agree with them?" Mr Crepsley howled.

"Actually," Seba replied, "I argued for change. But when the motion was defeated, I accepted it, as any loyal vampire would."

"The hell with loyalty!" Mr Crepsley barked. "If this is the price of loyalty, perhaps Kurda was right. Maybe it would have been for the best to turn this place over to the vampaneze!"

"You do not mean that," Seba smiled. "Step down, take your seat, and let Paris finish. You are making a fool of yourself."

"But—" Mr Crepsley began.

"Larten!" Seba snapped impatiently. "Down!"

Mr Crepsley's head dropped. "Very well," he sighed. "I shall bow to your will, and hear Paris out. But I am not leaving Darren's side, and any who tries to force me from this platform shall live to regret it."

"It is all right, Seba," Paris said as the quartermaster opened his mouth to argue. "Larten and the Little Person may remain." Once that had been settled, Paris continued with his speech. "As I said, we opted not to alter our laws. There may come a time when we have to, but we would rather not rush headlong into such a course of action. Change should be gradual. We must avoid panic and anarchy.

"Having agreed upon the need to be true to our laws, we searched for a loophole which Darren could take advantage of. Nobody in this Hall wished for his death. Even those most strenuously opposed to changes in the laws racked their brains in the hope that an escape clause would present itself.

"We considered the possibility of letting Darren 'escape' a second time, of relaxing the guard and allowing him to slip away with our unofficial blessing. But there would have been no honour in such a strategy. Darren would have been shamed; you, Larten, would have been shamed; and we who agreed to the compromise would also have been shamed.

"We decided against it."

Mr Crepsley bristled, then addressed the Princes in a hissed whisper. "Arra made me promise, on her deathbed, that I would not let Darren die. I beg you — do not force me to choose between loyalty to you and my vow to her."

"There will be no need to choose," Paris said. "There is no conflict of interests, as will become apparent as soon as you shut up and let me finish." He smiled as he said this. Then, raising his voice, he again addressed the Hall. "As those who were present during the debate know, Arrow was the first to suggest an honourable way out of our dilemma."

"I don't know how I thought of it," Arrow grunted, running a hand over his bald head, grimacing. "I've never been known as a great thinker. Normally, I act first and think later – if at all! – but a thought was swimming like a fish, deep within the ocean of my brain, and eventually it surfaced."

"The solution," Paris said, "is simplicity itself. We do not need to bend or change the laws to suit Darren's purposes. Instead, we need only place him above them."

"I do not understand," Mr Crepsley frowned.

"Think, Larten," Paris urged. "Who among us are immune to punishment? Who could fail the Trials of Initiation a dozen times and walk away untouched?"

Mr Crepsley's eyes widened. "You cannot mean...?" he gasped.

"We do," Paris smirked.

"But ... it is incomprehensible! He is too young! He is not a General! He is not even a full-vampire!"

"Who cares?" Mika Ver Leth chipped in, pulling a wry face. "We're not interested in the fine print. He's earned the right to bear the title. More than any of us here, perhaps, he is worthy."

"This is insane," Mr Crepsley said, but he was beginning to smile.

"Possibly," Paris agreed. "But it was put to a vote and all voted in favour of it."

"*All?*" Mr Crepsley blinked.

"Every single vampire in the Hall," Mika nodded.

"Excuse me," I whispered to Mr Crepsley, "but what's going on? What are you talking about?"

"Be quiet," he hushed me. "I will explain presently." He thought over the Princes' proposition – whatever it was – and his smile grew wider. "It makes sense, in a mad sort of way," he muttered. "But surely the title would be honorary? He knows so little of our ways, and he is so young and inexperienced."

"We would not expect him to engage in regular duties," Paris said. "He has much to learn and we will not rush his development. We will not even make a full-vampire of him — though we must share our blood, we will limit the amount, so he remains a half-vampire. But the appointment *will* be valid. He will not be a figurehead. He will hold all the responsibilities and powers of the post."

"Look," I grumbled, "tell me what's going on, or–" Mr Crepsley bent and whispered something in my ear. "What?" I snapped, and he whispered some more. "You can't be serious!" I yelped, feeling the blood rush from my face. "You're pulling my leg!"

"It is the only honourable way," he said.

"But … I couldn't … I'm not … I never…" I shook my head and stared around at the vampires packing the Hall of

Princes. They were all smiling now and nodding at me. Seba looked especially pleased. "That lot agreed to it?" I asked weakly.

"Every one of them," Paris said. "They respect you, Darren. They also admire you. What you have done for us shall never be forgotten as long as vampires walk the earth. We wish to show our appreciation, and this is the only way we know."

"I'm amazed," I mumbled. "I don't know what to say."

"Say 'Yes'," Arrow laughed, "or we'll have to take you down to the Hall of Death and punch a few holes in you!"

Looking up at Mr Crepsley, I squinted, then smiled. "You'd have to obey me if I went along with this, wouldn't you?" I asked.

"Of course," he grinned. "I and all others."

"You'd have to do whatever I said?"

"Yes." He lowered his voice. "But do not think you could push me around. I will respect your standing, but I will not let your head swell unchecked. You will still be my assistant and I will keep you in your rightful place!"

"I bet you will," I chuckled, then faced Paris and drew myself up straight. I stood on the verge of a monumental decision, which would change my life forever. I'd have liked a few nights to think about it, and dwell upon the consequences, but there was no time. It was this or the Hall of Death — and anything was preferable to being dropped on the vicious stakes! "What do I have to do?" I asked.

"There is a lengthy, involved ceremony," Paris said, "but that can be postponed until later. Right now all you need do is accept our blood and offer some of your own to the Stone of Blood. Once you have been recognized by the Stone, the deed is done and it can never be reversed."

"OK," I said nervously.

"Step forward then," Paris said, "and let the pact be sealed."

As I advanced, Mr Crepsley told Harkat what was going on, and I heard him exclaim, "No way!" I found it impossible to hide my grin during the ceremony, even though everybody else in the Hall remained solemn-faced.

First, I removed my top. Then Arrow, Mika and me gathered around the Stone of Blood (only two Princes were required for the ceremony). Using my sharp nails, I cut into the fleshy tips of my ten fingers, drawing blood. Arrow and Mika did the same. When we were ready, Arrow pressed the bloody fingertips of one of his hands to mine, and Mika did the same on the other side. Then the pair laid their free hands on the Stone of Blood, which glowed red and emitted a low thrumming noise.

I could feel the blood of the Princes flowing into me, and mine into them. It was an unpleasant sensation but it wasn't as painful as it had been when Mr Crepsley first blooded me all those years ago.

The Stone of Blood glowed brighter the longer we remained joined to it, and the outer rim became transparent, so that I was able to see inside it and watch as my blood was added to that of thousands of other creatures of the night.

Stray thoughts zipped frenziedly through my mind. I remembered the night when Mr Crepsley blooded me. My first real drink of blood, when Sam Grest lay dying in my arms. The vampaneze I'd killed in the cave. The mad vampaneze — Murlough. Steve Leopard — my best friend when I was a human, who'd sworn to track me down and kill me when he grew up. Debbie Hemlock and the softness of her lips when we kissed. Gavner — laughing. Mr Tall directing his performers at the Cirque Du Freak. Harkat telling me his name after we'd killed the rabid bear. Truska (the bearded lady) fitting me out in a pirate costume. Arra — winking. Mr Tiny with his heart-shaped watch and loveless eyes. Kurda facing the hall of vampires. Annie and how she used to tease me. Sticking stamps into albums with Mum. Pulling weeds in the garden with Dad. Gavner, Arra, Sam Grest — dying.

I grew faint and would have fallen, but Paris darted behind me and propped me up. The blood was flowing rapidly now, and so were the images. Faces from the past, friends and enemies, moving as fast as the frames of a movie, then faster. Just when I thought I couldn't stand any more, Arrow and Mika removed their hands from the Stone of Blood, then broke contact with me, signalling the end of the ceremony. As I slumped backwards, Paris quickly rubbed spit on to the tips of my fingers to stop the bleeding. "How do you feel?" he asked, checking my eyes.

"Weak," I muttered.

"Give it a few hours," he said. "Once the blood kicks in, you will feel like a panther!"

The sound of cheering reached my ears and I realized all the vampires in the hall were hollering their heads off. "What are they shouting about?" I asked.

"They want to see you," Paris said, smiling. "They wish to grant their approval."

"Can't they wait?" I asked. "I'm exhausted."

"We shall carry you," Paris said. "It would not do to keep your subjects waiting ... *Sire*."

"'Sire'," I repeated, and grinned, liking the sound of it.

The three Princes lifted me up and placed me lengthways on their shoulders. I laughed and stared at the ceiling as they carried me forward, marvelling at this bizarre twist of fate, wondering what the future would hold and if anything could ever compare with this.

As they put me down, so that I could take the applause of the vampires on my feet, I gazed around and noted the beaming faces of Mr Crepsley, Harkat, Seba Nile, Vanez Blane, and the others. At the back of the hall, I thought I spotted the ghostly shades of Gavner and Arra, and — just behind them — Kurda, applauding silently. But that must have been an effect of the dizziness caused by the addition of the Princes' blood.

Then the faces blurred and I was staring out upon a sea of yelling vampires, one the same as the next. Letting my eyes close, I stood there, shaky on my feet, rocking from the vibrations of their roars, proud as a peacock, listening numbly as they chanted my name and cheered for me — me ... Darren Shan ... *the Vampire Prince*!

TO BE CONTINUED...

THE SAGA CONTINUES...

HUNTERS
OF THE DUSK

BY DAWN we knew we had a fight on our hands. We were being followed, not just by one person, but three or four. They'd picked up our trail a few kilometres outside the town and had been tracking us ever since. They moved with admirable stealth, and if we hadn't been anticipating trouble, we might not have known anything was amiss. But when a vampire senses danger, not even the most fleet-footed human can sneak up on him.

"What's the plan?" Harkat asked as we were making camp in the middle of a small forest, sheltered from the sun beneath the intertwining branches and leaves.

"They will wait for full daylight to attack," Mr Crepsley said, keeping his eyes low and his voice lower. "We will act as though all is normal and pretend to sleep. When they come, we deal with them."

"Will you be OK in the sun?" I asked. Though we were sheltered where we were, a battle might draw us out of the shade.

"The rays will not harm me during the short time it will take to deal with these stalkers," Mr Crepsley replied.

Making beds for ourselves amid the moss and leaves on the ground, we wrapped ourselves in our cloaks and settled down. "Of course, they might just be curious," Harkat muttered. "They could simply want to see ... what a real-life vampire looks like."

"They move too keenly to be mere spectators," Mr

Crepsley disagreed. "They are here on business."

"I just remembered," I hissed. "The guy in the shop was buying *guns!*"

"Most vampire hunters come properly armed," Mr Crepsley grunted. "Gone are the nights when the fools toted only a hammer and wooden stake."

There was no more talk after that. We lay still, eyes closed (except for Harkat, who covered his lidless eyes with his cloak), breathing evenly, feigning sleep.

Seconds passed slowly, taking an age to become minutes, and an eternity to become hours. It had been six years since my last taste of vicious combat. My limbs felt unnaturally cold, and stiff icy snakes of fear coiled and uncoiled inside the walls of my stomach. I kept flexing my fingers beneath the folds of my cloak, never far from my sword, ready to draw.

Shortly after midday, the hunters moved in for the kill. There were three of them, spread out in a semicircle, coming at us from the north, southwest and southeast. At first I could only hear the rustling of leaves as they approached, and the occasional snap of a twig. But as they closed upon us, I became aware of their heavy breathing, the creaks of their tense bones, the pacy, panicked pounding of their hearts.

The hunters came to a standstill ten or twelve metres away, tucked behind trees, preparing themselves to attack. There was a long, nervous pause — then the sound of a gun being slowly cocked.

"*Now!*" Mr Crepsley roared, springing to his feet, launching himself at the human nearest him.

While Mr Crepsley closed upon his assailant at incredible speed, Harkat and me targeted the other two humans. The one I'd set my sights on cursed loudly, stepped out from behind his tree, brought his rifle up and fired. A bullet whizzed past me, missing by several centimetres. Before he could fire again, I was upon him.

I wrenched the rifle from the human's hands and tossed it away. A gun went off behind me, but it was fired almost straight into the air, and I guessed Harkat must be grappling with his foe. There was no time to check on my friend – the man in front of me had already drawn a long hunting knife – so I slid my sword out ready for action.

The man's eyes widened when he saw the sword – he'd painted the area around his eyes with red circles of what looked like blood – then narrowed. "You're just a kid," he snarled, slashing at me with his knife.

"No," I disagreed, stepping out of range of his knife, jabbing at him with my sword. "I'm much more."

As the human slashed at me again, I brought my sword up and out in a smooth arcing slice, through the flesh, muscles and bones of his right hand, severing three of his fingers, disarming him in an instant.

The human cried out in agony and fell away from me. I took advantage of the moment to see how Mr Crepsley and Harkat were faring. Mr Crepsley had already despatched his human, and was striding towards Harkat, who was wrestling with his opponent. Harkat appeared to have the advantage of his foe, but Mr Crepsley was moving into place to back him up should the battle take a turn for the worse.

Satisfied that all was going in our favour, I switched my attention back to the man on the ground, psyching myself up for the unpleasant task of making an end of him. To my surprise, I found him grinning horribly at me.

"You should have taken my other hand too!" he growled.

My eyes fixed on the man's left hand and my breath caught in my throat — he was clutching a hand-grenade close to his chest!

"Don't move!" he shouted as I lurched towards him. He half-pressed down on the detonator with his thumb. "If this goes off, it takes you with me!"

DARREN SHAN
CIRQUE DU FREAK

**THE SAGA OF DARREN SHAN
BOOK 1**

Darren Shan is just an ordinary schoolboy – until he gets an invitation to visit the Cirque Du Freak... until he meets Madam Octa... until he comes face to face with a creature of the night.

Soon, Darren and his friend Steve are caught in a deadly trap. Darren must make a bargain with the one person who can save Steve. But that person is not human and only deals in blood...

ISBN 978 0 00 675416 9

www.darrenshan.com

DARREN SHAN

THE
VAMPIRE'S ASSISTANT

THE SAGA OF DARREN SHAN
BOOK 2

Darren Shan was just an ordinary schoolboy – until his visit to the Cirque Du Freak. Now, as he struggles with his new life as a Vampire's Assistant, he tries desperately to resist the one thing that can keep him alive… blood. But a gruesome encounter with the Wolf Man may change all that…

ISBN 978 0 00 675513 9

www.darrenshan.com

DARREN SHAN

TUNNELS OF BLOOD

THE SAGA OF DARREN SHAN
BOOK 3

Darren Shan, the Vampire's Assistant, get's a taste of city life when he leaves the Cirque Du Freak with Evra and Mr Crepsley. At night the vampire goes about secret business, while by day Darren enjoys his freedom.

But then bodies are discovered... Corpses drained of blood... The hunt for the killer is on and Darren's loyalties are tested to the limit as he fears the worst. One mistake and they are all doomed to perish in the tunnels of blood...

ISBN 978 0 00 675514 2

www.darrenshan.com

DARREN SHAN
VAMPIRE MOUNTAIN

THE SAGA OF DARREN SHAN
BOOK 4

Darren Shan and Mr Crepsley embark on a dangerous
trek to the very heart of the vampire world. But they
face morethan the cold on Vampire Mountain – the
vampaneeze have been there before them...

Will a meeting with the Vampire Princes restore
Darren's human side, or turn him further towards the
darkness? Only one thing is certain – Darren's
initiation into the vampire clan is more deadly than
he can ever have imagined.

ISBN 978 0 00 711441 2

www.darrenshan.com

DARREN SHAN

TRIALS OF DEATH

THE SAGA OF DARREN SHAN
BOOK 5

The Trials: seventeen ways to die unless the luck of
the vampires is with you. Darren Shan must pass five
fearsome Trials to prove himself to the vampire clan —
or face the stakes in the Hall of Death.

But Vampire Mountain holds hidden threats.
Sinister, potent forces are gathering in the darkness.
In this nightmare world of bloodshed and betrayal,
death may be a blessing...

ISBN 978 0 00 711440 5

www.darrenshan.com

DARREN SHAN